THE PROMOTION

A REVERSE HAREM ROMANCE

MIKA LANE

HEADLANDS PUBLISHING

Copyright© 2018 by Mika Lane
Headlands Publishing
4200 Park Blvd. #244
Oakland, CA 94602

The Promotion is a work of fiction. Names, characters, (most) places, and incidents are either the product of the author's creativity or are used fictitiously. Any resemblance to actual persons, living or dead, events, or locales is entirely coincidental.
All rights reserved. This book or any portion thereof may not be reproduced or used in any manner whatsoever without the express written permission of the publisher except for the use of quotations in a book review.

BE THE FIRST TO KNOW...

Want more heat, heart,
and bad boys who know what they're doing?
Join my list and I'll send the steam straight to your inbox,
starting with a deliciously naughty story:

MAIZY

DEAR EMPLOYEE:

As the end of this quarter approaches, that means it's time for your annual performance review. Please complete the form attached, describing your top three accomplishments of the past year, and return it to your manager. He/she will contact you to discuss this in the next four weeks. And, as always, thank you for making our law firm one of the best in New York City...

Oh, boy. My favorite time of the year. The one where my boss had the opportunity to remind me of all the times that, in her eyes, I had failed her and would never, ever amount to much of anything, never mind get the promotion I was jonesing for.

How did I end up in a reality where someone else—someone I didn't even like or respect—had so much control over my life?

It wasn't obvious from the beginning what I'd signed up for when I'd joined the firm. From the start, she was nice as could be, interested in who I was, complimentary about the work I did, telling me she liked my dresses. Then, slowly, slowly the insults and jabs started. They were so tiny at first, I almost didn't notice them. But when they escalated to full-on bitchery, well, then I had to admit I'd gotten on the wrong damn train.

The way it sneaked up on me was like that fable about the boiling frog. The water temperature increased too slowly to perceive any danger—the poor bastard didn't realize he was burning up until it was too late.

Or something like that.

I guess everyone who worked and had a boss was in the same boat, at least to some extent. Vulnerable to the whims of someone else's moods, personality, impulses. It was a total crapshoot, wasn't it? You could get a good boss who gave a damn about you or some psycho who lived to destroy your soul.

And they say the white-collar world was civilized? I'd never seen people act more like disgusting beasts.

Actual animals in the wild were kinder and more logical than some of the people I'd worked with.

But that wasn't to say *everyone* I worked with was an asshole. Just *a lot* of them. And that was partly because I worked at a law firm. Everyone knew law firms attracted more than their share of dick heads. But in spite of that, I did have a couple work friends, thank god. We helped each other get through the weeks, as the weeks turned into years.

My buddy, Cato, was one of the firm's junior partners. We started about the same time, and even though I was on the paralegal team and he was one of the attorneys, he never acted like he was better than me. Yeah, law firms have these insane hierarchies, with the lawyers at the top, as you might imagine. Then come the paralegals like me, and the admins who, if they were real assholes, picked on the poor slobs in the law library or mailroom.

I guess what it boils down to is that everyone has their bitch.

Who would the mailroom people pick on at the end of one of their bad days? Maybe they went home and kicked their dogs.

God, I hoped not.

Anyway, I didn't have time to focus on that. I had a party to get to.

"Sparkle!" I hollered after I unlocked the front door to the apartment I shared with my sister.

Silence. Shit, I needed her to help me decide what to wear.

So I poked my head into her room where I found her sitting cross-legged on the floor, butt naked, wearing huge headphones, and chanting *ommm*. She'd finish one round, take a deep breath, and begin another *ommm*. In the corner of the room her pet rat, Cher, rustled around the newspaper lining in his cage.

Her eyes were closed, and she looked so damn peaceful that I wasn't sure I should interrupt. But she could meditate any time. I, on the other hand, rarely had a social engagement with the sort of expectations that came with a party for my law firm's fiftieth anniversary. This was the big time. And it was happening in two hours.

"Sparkle," I called, as if she'd be able to hear me through her headphones.

Ommm…

C'mon, sis.

I walked up behind her and pulled off her headphones.

"What the hell!" she yelled. So much for meditative peacefulness.

"Spark, I have that work thing tonight. You're helping me, right?"

"Oh, that's right." She stood up, her skinny little naked body toned and lithe from all the yoga classes she taught.

"Let's go dig into your closet," she said, heading toward my bedroom.

"Spark, put something on first."

She looked down at herself with the same surprise as if I'd told her she was green.

"Oh, okay. Right." She grabbed her purple plushy robe. It made her look like a tall, thin stuffed Barney.

"THIS IS A BIG NIGHT, SPARK," I told her as she carefully applied my eyeshadow.

"Yeah?"

"Well, our annual reviews are coming up, and I'm hoping this is my year to be promoted to senior paralegal."

"Oh, right. That's so cool."

"Yeah. I'd get paid more, I'd get more responsibility, and maybe even could work for a different attorney than the bitch I currently am trapped under. So tonight, I plan to impress."

"I'm sure you will," she said. "Take a look in the mirror."

Wow. I barely recognized myself.

"Sure you don't want some glittery false eyelashes?" she offered.

"Thanks, Spark. But this is a law firm party, not Burning Man."

Before I entered the fancy ballroom for our fancy party, I took a quick sec to make sure there was no lipstick on my teeth. And, glancing around to make sure no one would see, I also re-adjusted the girls to make sure I had a little—but not too much—cleavage showing. Attractive, but not too attractive. That seemed to be the way it worked at a law firm.

I entered the party with a big smile on my face, as if I did things like this all the time. Like I was some sort of movie star whom people would be thrilled to see walk through the door. Camera-ready, as they say.

But in reality, all that happened were a few heads turned my way, and then turned right back to the other heads they were clustered with.

Fuckers.

I didn't let that deter me. I might be a mid-level paralegal who'd only attended a crummy state college, but I was going to be somebody people respected. And admired. And wanted to party with.

I made my way toward the bar, always the safe first stop at any party, while my eyes scanned the crowd for my buddy Cato. We'd agreed to meet there and help each other suffer through any indignities. I ordered a gin and tonic—a work party seemed a bit too formal for a beer—and walked over to the group Cato was chatting with.

They were all drinking beer.

Anyway, when I got close enough, I inched my way into the circle, lightly rubbing my arm against Cato to let him know I was there and to make room for me.

"Maizy!" he exclaimed like he'd never been so glad to see someone. Cato was great that way, always knowing just how to make someone feel special.

"Hi, everyone," I said, continuing to beam my bright smile. "What a party!" I looked around the room in awe. What an actress.

"Does everyone know Maizy?" Cato asked. "She's one of our top paralegals. We're very lucky to have her." Shit. I'd have to buy him lunch for that.

"Oh, Cato, that's so nice of you," I gushed.

The others in the group nodded at me, murmuring a few hellos, before they turned back to their lawyer talk. There were a couple glances at my cleavage, though.

Ugh. Was I showing too much?

Oh, no. My boss was heading right for me.

"Maizy," she said, touching my arm. As if she liked me. Which I was pretty sure she didn't.

"Eva! Wow, I love your dress." It *was* a nice dress. Probably cost a thousand dollars, unlike mine, which came from the sale rack at Ann Taylor.

"Let's walk, shall we?" she asked, leading me away from the safety blanket that was Cato. Did she really want to hang out with me? Maybe she had something important to talk about and realized what an excellent confidante I would be.

I was finally getting the recognition I deserved.

As Eva steered me through the crowd, she occasionally nodded and shook the hand of another guest. She didn't bother to introduce me, which I would have found insulting if I hadn't believed she and I were about to have a real, personal conversation.

When we were far enough from the other party-goers that no one could hear us, she looked at me with that cat smile, the one where I never knew if she was going to compliment my work or tear it to shreds. It was quite a skill to keep someone on the brink of a panic attack. I wondered where she'd become so practiced.

"Maizy, you look so pretty tonight. All that… eyeshadow. It's so…glittery."

"Oh, thanks, Eva, my sister helped me—"

"Right," she interrupted before I could tell her about Sparkle's awesome makeup skills. "Maizy, have you noticed some of the partners' wives here tonight have not been exactly…um, friendly?"

Of course I had. Did she think I was freaking blind? But the old bitches were always like that.

"Oh, well yeah. But they're never friendly to me. It's the funniest thing," I babbled.

"Maizy, did it occur to you to wonder why these women are not friendly to you? And why, at an event like this, the men aren't that friendly to you either?"

I finally realized she'd not pulled me aside for a friendly conversation, but something more sinister. I waited for her to sink her fangs into me and to inject just enough venom to leave me doubting myself for the next decade of my life.

Because I knew it was coming.

"I'm sharing this with you because your review is coming up, and I know you're hoping for that promotion to senior paralegal."

Oh, god. What was she getting at?

"Um, right," I said, forcing some steadiness into my voice.

"Maizy," she said, looking around again to make sure no one could hear us, "it's because you're single that people aren't friendly to you."

"Huh?" I wasn't usually that inarticulate with my boss, but at that moment, the words were just not coming.

"You see, you're young and beautiful, and dare I say, sexy? The wives don't particularly like their husbands around someone like you. And the men feel like they have to steer clear."

I swallowed hard, a sip of my gin and tonic having done nothing to help the strangled sensation in my throat.

"If you really want to move up in the firm…"

She waited, it seemed to make sure I was listening carefully, so I nodded like a bobble-head.

"You need to have a husband."

Wha…?

Did she really say what I thought she did?

"Or, at least a fiancé," she added quickly. "You see, at a conservative firm like ours, young women like… you…are a threat to some people. And unfortunately, those are the people who carry a lot of weight."

"S…so I…um…would have a more successful career if I had a boyfriend?"

She pursed her lips while she looked at me, which I didn't know was possible with all the Botox it was rumored she got. "Not just a boyfriend, Maizy. A fiancé or even better, a husband."

She waved across the room at some woman and put her hand back on my arm.

"I'm so glad we got to have this talk, Maizy. Please do think about what I said." And she was off, floating across the room to talk to someone undoubtedly more important than me.

And who probably had a fiancé. Or even a husband.

2

ANSON

I CAME UP OUT OF THE SUBWAY AT 59TH STREET AND Columbus Circle and headed over to my brother and sister-in-law's place for another of their insufferable dinner parties. I usually managed to avoid them with any number of lame excuses they'd accept, but tonight was different. Eva, my brother's wife, would not let me off the hook.

She had someone from her firm she wanted me to meet. And Eva got what Eva wanted.

So to protest in my best passive-aggressive fashion, I was not only twenty minutes late but also arrived empty-handed—no wine, no flowers, no nothing. I hoped they wouldn't tell my mother, who'd kill me for my rudeness.

The last time Eva tried to set me up with someone,

it had been worse than disastrous. The woman was nice enough, even a good time. She'd come home with me after our first date, which I thought was a nice bonus. Boy, did that blow up in my face.

You see, I didn't call her again. Yeah, she slept with me and all, but in New York, there are tons of beautiful women. You hardly ever go out with anyone for a second time. My bad.

A couple days after our date, she started calling me. And I guess, as a dick move on my part, I ignored her messages. That's when they started coming in more frequently. And that's when I realized I was in trouble.

My date told Eva and her husband—my brother— that I'd fucked her and never called her again.

Who does that?

And boy, was I in the doghouse with them for a while. But it was actually a sort of blessing. It meant Eva was off my back.

After that, she'd given up on me for a good year or two. But it didn't last. Like the true matchmaking addict that she was, she slowly fell back into it, like a repeat offender.

No more sleeping with blind dates though, I told myself, no matter how aggressively they might grab my crotch during the cab ride home. You just don't know who might turn out to be a psycho these days. Or tell your family about your man-whore tendencies.

I took a deep breath before walking up the steps to

Eva and Todd's building. *God, please don't let this one be a weirdo.*

"Ans, buddy, great to see you," Todd said, giving me the male one-armed hug that guys did.

"Yo," I said in a whisper while we were still in the foyer. "Is it bad? Is she a freak? Dude, I gotta know. I can't take another psycho."

Todd burst out laughing, like the dick brother that he was. When the drama went down with the blind date from a couple years ago, he actually told my parents, if you can believe that.

Yes, even my parents found out I'd fucked a girl on the first date and then not called her. As you might imagine, I avoided them for a while, too.

"Dude, there's nothing to worry about. C'mon." He took a step back and looked at me, head cocked. He jiggled the ice cubes in whatever amber liquid he was drinking and pulled me into the living room.

"Get me one of what you're drinking, or I'll kill you," I hissed.

Eva came swanning from across the room. That's what she did—swanned. I'm not sure that was a real word or one I'd made up, but she floated toward me with her neck arched high and her arms spread in preparation for the world's most dramatic hug.

Which was weird because she basically hated me.

"My little brother, Anson," she purred. She took me in her giant wingspan and whispered in my ear, "You better not screw this one up."

She pulled back and looked at me with this beatific smile. I glanced around to see if anyone else knew what a devil she was, but she had them all fooled, it seemed.

She took my hand in her scratchy, bony one, and pulled me into the room. I scanned the place as subtly as possible, trying to determine who was to be my not-so-discreet fix-up. Before I could make a full assessment, she'd plopped me in front of the woman whom I guessed was to be my date.

Was she kidding?

This woman was goddamn gorgeous. I breathed a sigh of relief and extended my hand to a tall, curvy blonde with glasses.

"Oh, hi," she said, yanking them off. I never understood why women were so embarrassed about glasses. "I'm Maizy." She extended her hand and laid a smile on me that just about knocked me over.

Eva beamed, obviously pleased with her match, and certain I'd never again fuck one of her set-ups on the first date. Yeah, I'd be paying for that mistake for the rest of my days.

Eva scurried off, probably to watch from a distance. That's how she was.

"I'm…uh…Anson."

Holy shit. *This* was what the law firms were producing these days? My new friend took a draw on her wine, but she looked longingly at my bourbon.

"You like bourbon? You want some?" I asked, gesturing at the bar.

She looked around sneakily. "I'd better not. At least not yet."

There was fear in her voice. She knew what my sister-in-law was all about, clearly.

I led her to a small sofa. A strategic move—no one else could sit with us.

"So you're a lawyer, huh? At my sister-in-law's firm?" God, she had great legs. I hoped she wasn't a bitch like Eva.

"Oh, no! Hell, no." As soon as she said it, she clapped her hand over her mouth. Her eyes scanned the room again, like she was in enemy territory.

Christ, who'd traumatized this woman?

She leaned closer. Her hair, which was piled on top of her head in a messy knot thing, smelled great.

"I'm not an attorney. Just a paralegal." She straightened her back and lifted her chin. "Yes, I'm a paralegal, I mean. Sorry. Didn't mean to say *just*."

"Awesome, I'm *glad* you're not a goddamn attorney." *Oops.* It was my turn to look around the room as if the firing squad were warming up. "I mean, not that there's anything wrong with it."

She snickered conspiratorially and clinked her glass against mine.

"I thought you were going to be some uptight attorney like all Eva's other friends. I mean, look around this room. Must have the biggest proportion of dick heads of any party going on in Manhattan at this very moment."

She pressed her lips together, but a laugh escaped anyway. She threw her head back, cracking up. The whole room turned to look at her. I supposed that was a too-loud laugh for the sensibilities of the others. But I freaking loved it.

Eva called everyone to the table, and of course, she was the type of hostess who told everyone where to sit. Regardless, some other sap was trying to grab the seat right next to Maizy, but I cock-blocked him big time.

"Ugh, sorry, dude. This is my seat," I told him as I set my ass in it. Maizy didn't notice a thing as she gently put a white linen napkin on her lap. The other dude might have scowled for all I knew, but with my back to him, I had no idea. And couldn't have cared less.

"Have you been here before, Maizy? To Eva and Todd's?" I asked.

"Nooo," she replied, shaking her head. She leaned a bit closer, which I liked. "I was shocked I was invited. I'm pretty sure Eva doesn't like me. In fact, I'm absolutely sure she doesn't like me." She shrugged. Apparently, she didn't lose much sleep over Eva. Neither did I, but then, she wasn't my boss.

"You know, Maizy, you need to be sure to give me your number before the evening is over."

"I might be able to do that," she said with that goddamn killer smile.

Shit.

THE PROMOTION

17

3

———————

MAIZY

HOW FREAKING WEIRD WAS IT TO BE INVITED TO MY boss's house for dinner? The woman usually acted like I had the plague, as if spending too much time with a commoner like me would tarnish her Harvard pedigree.

Her friends weren't much better. So when her brother-in-law arrived, I nearly cried with joy. Someone who wanted to talk to me.

I'd taken Eva's suggestions to heart and dressed as unsexily as I could. I even wore my glasses instead of my contacts, but the women in the room still eyed me warily as the only single.

I wouldn't have minded giving those bitches something to really talk about.

But Anson. Wow. He was nothing like his short, bald brother Todd, beleaguered spouse of Eva the evil. No, the family must have spent all their good looks karma on the younger brother Anson, because there was pretty much nothing about him that was less than perfect with his unkempt red hair and facial scruff. He reminded me of that prince of England, whose name I could never remember, but whom I'd had a crush on since I was a kid.

Eva's server—yes, she had a fucking server for her dinner party—brought us our soup. Mine was a strange watery concoction with a carrot floating in it, but it was surprisingly tasty.

Anson leaned closer to me.

"She always makes shit like this. And brings in maids. So idiotic," he whispered.

It was then that my shoulders began to shake. Then my hands, so I set down my soup spoon. I pressed my hand over my mouth to control my laughter, but the harder I tried not to laugh, the worse it was.

Didn't they call that the *church giggles*?

Anson was watching me struggling to keep my shit together, when he, too, was struck with laughter. His face turned beet red, and his blue eyes filled with tears.

"Hey, guys," Eva called out. "Why don't you share the joke with us?"

She had no idea how that would fuck up her evening. So we didn't.

I cleared my throat and pushed my chair from the

table. "Excuse me. I'll be right back." I scurried to the restroom. I felt bad about abandoning Anson, but at this point, it was every woman for herself. He was related to those people. He would do whatever the hell he wanted. I, on the other hand, could not. I had to deal with Eva at work on Monday. The harder I laughed, the worse it would be. That's how she was.

I ran into the restroom and took a few deep breaths to shake off my nerves.

There was a knock at the bathroom door.

Shit, didn't this place have more than one bathroom?

"Maizy?" a muffled voice said. "Maizy, you okay?"

I yanked open the door to Anson.

"God, I'm sorry. I just couldn't take it. I guess I was nervous, and that set me off." I stepped out of the bathroom and joined him in the hall, taking several more deep breaths.

"Whew. I'm fine now," I said, moving back toward the dining room.

But before I could, Anson's hand grabbed my wrist.

"What are you—?"

His lips brushed over mine, quietly and gently, as if asking permission. I was shocked as hell, but hey, he was a nice-looking guy, and according to Eva, I was the resident floozy anyway.

"Hmmm, mmmm," came the throat-clearing sound from behind me.

Anson and I snapped back from each other, and I

gestured toward his mouth so he could remove the red lipstick I'd smeared on him.

Eva stood there with a smug look on her face. I couldn't tell if she was disgusted with me or pleased with her matchmaking skills. Maybe it was a bit of both.

"Hey, Eva. We're heading back to the table," Anson said. He still had a smudge of red on his upper lip.

"Good," she said, looking from one of us to the other. "Dessert is being served."

I smiled brightly at her as we headed back to the table, laughing fits long gone.

"SHARE A CAB HOME?" Anson asked as the evening ended with everyone heading for the door at once. Geez, it seemed like they couldn't wait to get the hell out of there.

"Heading across town?" I asked.

"I am. Let me call at Uber."

Our ride sped through several red lights on the way to my place. Just another night in Manhattan.

"Would you like to get together again, Maizy?"

Oh, shit. I'd thought that moment might be coming. And I'd not come up with a good response. What the hell. Honesty it would be.

"You know, Anson, thank you. I'm super flattered—"

"Oooh, that doesn't sound positive."

"Yeah. Sorry." I nodded. "I feel a little weird about dating one of my boss's relatives."

Perfectly legit reasoning.

"Okay. I get that. I really do. But look at it this way. Neither of us can stand her. I mean, I only tolerate Todd because he's my brother. But he's as big an elitist asshole lawyer as she is."

Oh, god. He was going to wear me down. Not that it was hard to do.

He turned in his seat to face me. "So the way I look at it, Maizy, is that if we don't stick together, we'll be eaten alive by these jerks. We need to partner. In solidarity."

I looked at him to see if he was serious. We burst out laughing.

"I'll think about it, Anson. Really, thank you. Put your number in my phone, would you?"

He got the Uber driver to wait while he walked me up to the door.

"I don't even know what you do for work," I said.

"Oh. Finance. You know that gig. Not quite as cliché as a lawyer. But I suppose we're getting there."

Not quite as cliché as the single femme fatale in the office, either. But I was dealing with it, nonetheless.

AFTER ALL THE excitement of having been to my boss's house, I couldn't wait to fall into bed. Before I did, I went to fetch the usual glass of water for my nightstand. And who was standing there in the middle of the kitchen but my sister Sparkle. Naked, of course. Holding her pet rat.

"Spark, why can't you wear clothes in the house?"

I don't think I really cared that she walked around naked. It just seemed like since I was the big sister, I should say something about it.

Maybe I was the jerk. Maybe I had an issue with nudity.

"Maiz," she started, "I swear, if you walk around the house naked once in a while, you'll understand why I do. It's so freeing."

Not sure I bought it.

"Here. Say hi to Cher." She thrust the little white rat in my face. I had to admit, he was cute. Even though he had a woman's name and dropped little brown turdlettes all over the place every time Sparkle let him out of his cage.

Anyway.

"So, I survived the dinner," I said.

Sparkle's head snapped in my direction.

"Right! Tell me!"

"She wanted me to meet a guy. Her brother-in-law."

I shook my head. Saying it out loud kind of creeped me out. Dating someone related to my boss? It would be weird if she were nice, but considering I wasn't her biggest fan, and I was pretty sure she didn't like me either, it was downright gross.

"And?" Sparkle asked.

"He was pretty cool. Very nice looking."

"Wow. Score. What's not to like?"

"Ugh, not sure about dating him. But I do want to find someone. Apparently, being single is holding me back professionally."

"What?"

"Yeah. I didn't tell you? Eva took me aside at the big party for the firm and told me I was a threat to the wives since I was young and single."

"She. Did. Not."

"Can you believe that shit? I mean, what is this, the nineteen-fifties? Now I'm the office hussy." I headed for my bed, and Sparkle followed. Naked, of course. Cher ran across my bed, dropping a tiny poop.

"Spark, can you believe someone would look down on me because I'm not paired off? Such a bunch of judgmental fucks."

"Ugh. Terrible. I don't know how you can stand that profession. Lawyers suck. Hey, you could always become a yoga teacher like me, you know," she said.

"Yeah, and then I could change my name to something like Sparkle, right?"

She rolled her eyes. "Sparkle suits me much better than that stupid name I had before."

"I don't know. I never thought *Sunday* was such a bad name," I said. "Anyway, one of us has to have a real job. How the hell would we pay the rent?"

"Hey, no fair. I help with the bills." She gave me her little sister pout. "Oh. I know what you should do. I have an idea."

She bounced on her toes and waved her arms wildly.

"Okay. What's your idea?"

"They have those matchmaking agencies." She jumped from the bed and ran toward her room, her naked butt jiggling the tiniest bit. Ten seconds later, she returned to my room with her laptop.

"I'm pulling one of the sites up right now. Okay, here's one that's local and it has good reviews. It's called VIP Match."

"But I'm not a VIP."

She perused the webpage. "I don't think you have to be a VIP. Let's see...Oh. Shit. It costs five thousand dollars."

"*What?*" Who would spend five thousand dollars to get a date?

Apparently, enough people to keep VIP Match in business.

"Forget them. Not worth five thousand dollars." She clicked on her keyboard, presumably scrolling through all the possibilities.

"Hey, here's one where the guy pays."

"Are you sure that's not an escort service?" I asked.

She clicked several more times.

"Ummm…yeah, looks like it is," she said. "Sorry."

"Hey, maybe I should give it a shot. I could make some money and get my promotion at the same time."

Well, that was one option.

4

BRADEN

I don't know what I hated more—lawyers, or the freaking awful offices they worked in. All kinds of fake wood paneling, furniture from my grandmother's era, and oriental carpets. Law firms must have been single-handedly keeping rug stores open.

Then came the stuffy, stuck-up attitudes. It started with the people behind the front desk. When I first started having to hire attorneys, like when my music began to take off, I'd walk in and, of course, I stuck out like a sore thumb among all the suits. I mean, every profession has its uniform, and mine was worn Levi's, some sort of old concert T-shirt, and a leather jacket with a hoodie underneath. If it was really cold, I'd bust out the down puffer.

I almost felt sorry for the attorneys and all their

workers having to wear those fucking monkey suits. They looked so uncomfortable and…expensive. What if a little of your lunch spilled down the front of one of those jackets? If good old mister dry cleaner couldn't work one of his miracles and get the stain out, you were screwed out of a couple thousand bucks.

Not that I couldn't afford to dress that way if I wanted to. I could buy any of those fuckers at that firm ten times over if I wanted to. But I was practical. I wore clothes I didn't have to worry about. If I spilled on them, or left them behind in some hotel room, it didn't matter.

I simply did not give a shit.

I had bigger things to worry about. Like my fucking music label licensing my work for a fucking car commercial. I was seriously so steamed about that, I couldn't see straight. And when I had an issue like this, the lawyers usually came to *me* for our meetings. But my schedule had been so whacked with the release of my new album that I broke down and went to their offices for a change. I also felt a little bad I'd canceled on them so many times.

But just a little. I paid those fuckers through the nose. They could kiss my ass once in a while.

So. Back in a law office. I'd forgotten how much I hated them. I'd always felt these leeches made money off the back of other peoples' hard work. But they could come in handy once when you needed them.

"Mr. Darby?" a hot-as-shit tall blonde asked me. "I'm Maizy Strong."

"Call me Braden." I stood and took her hand. Damn if she wasn't almost as tall as me with her skyscraper heels. And I was six-foot.

"Actually, call me Brade."

I followed the sexy secretary down a long hall past a bunch of dickwad lawyer offices to a conference room with windows featuring a view of the whole of lower Manhattan. I knew without a doubt I was paying for that view with the monthly fees they charged me. At least I got to enjoy it for the hour I was there.

I was surprised when Mary—or whatever her name was—sat down with me at the huge conference table. Secretaries usually made themselves scarce after offering coffee or water. But, hey, I didn't mind this looker keeping me occupied until my lawyer came in.

In fact, what a great idea. Keep the dudes happy in the company of a beautiful female, and meetings were always sure to go well.

But my sexy secretary didn't offer me anything to drink. In fact, she pulled some big black eye glasses off the top of the hair piled on her head and opened the folder she'd had tucked under her arm. Out came a pen from behind her ear, and she took a long look at me.

"I've been a fan of your band's since I was in middle school," she said.

Shit. Way to make a guy feel ancient.

"That's very nice of you to say." Always be polite with the fans. Even if you are paying them.

She flipped through some papers.

"Mr. Darby—I mean, Brade—your case is pretty straightforward. We've handled a couple similar ones for other entertainers. The rulings have always been in favor of our clients, so you're in good hands."

"Um…excuse me, Marcy, I think you said?"

"Maizy. M-A-I-Z-Y."

"Ah. Gotcha. Maizy. I believe I had a meeting scheduled with a lawyer-type person. I appreciate your keeping me company, but I don't really have time to hang out with a secretary. Nothing personal, I hope you understand."

Huh. Well, I guess she didn't understand because she gave me the stink-eye of all stink-eyes. I bet if I hadn't been a client, she would have told me to go fuck myself.

I wouldn't have minded. I'd been told that before.

She placed her hand flat on the table on top of what I guessed was a folder of my problems and rolled her shoulders a bit. Kind of like she was getting ready for a fight.

Oh, shit. Guess I'd said the wrong thing.

"Look, Marcy—"

"I'm Maizy, sir. Maizy. I'm sorry about the misunderstanding, but I am your legal representative. I work under the supervision of Eva Crabtree, one of the firm's senior partners. I will be handling your case at the preliminary stages."

Oh. Shit.

She continued. "You and I will be working closely together, but if you're not comfortable with the arrangement and would prefer another paralegal, that can be arranged."

"Oh. Okay, cool, Maizy." I was sure to say it slowly and carefully. "Let's do it."

"You sure?" she asked.

I sat back in my seat and sized her up. I felt bad about insulting her.

"I am very sorry," I said.

"It's okay." The ramrod stiffness holding her up relaxed a bit, and the air in the room flowed again. "Now, shall we get started?"

We went back and forth for about twenty minutes. She asked me a million questions about the complaint I had against the record label, and then we poured over the massive stack of different contracts I had with them.

Shit, why wasn't my manager handling this for me?

Because he was the one who got me into this situation to begin with. I could strangle the jerk. As it was, I'd avoided his calls and texts for two weeks. That's how pissed I was with him. I'd talk to him again, eventually, but not until I was damn good and ready.

And I kind of liked knowing he was probably sweating his job. That would teach him to sell me out.

To be honest, legal talk bored me to tears. I mean, didn't it bore everyone? Except lawyers? And paralegals, I supposed. While Maizy jabbered on concerning some shit I could have cared less about—just get me the results I wanted—I had the chance to admire her.

She was fucking beautiful with her perfect skin and high cheekbones. I loved that she had this mass of sexy blonde hair, but that she had those heavy, dark nerd glasses that were so in vogue.

If anyone had told me a few years ago that hot blondes would someday be wearing those specs, I never would have believed it.

Her dress was this light blue color, nice and snug from what I could see, with long, fitted sleeves. Her tits strained against the fabric, and while I tried my damnedest not to stare, every time she looked down at her papers, my gaze wandered back to them.

She closed her folder and leaned back in her chair.

Was she finally going to lighten up a bit?

Wonder if she wanted to get a drink later? Eh, she was probably married to some asshole lawyer. Or doctor.

"Thanks for this info, Brade. I think you have a strong case. We're going to take good care of you. The brands using your music will have to stop, but they'll also expect their money back from the royalties they paid. If all goes according to plan, the record label will have to absorb that."

Yes.

I extended my hand. "Thank you. And again, sorry I didn't know who you were at first."

She shrugged. "That's okay. It happens." She stood to escort me out.

"You know, I was in a band in college," she said.

Holy fuck.

Was she kidding?

"Get outta here," I said, nodding. "That's pretty badass. I didn't know lawyer types—I mean, paralegal types—were rockers."

"Well, Brade, you don't know much about people in the legal profession, do you?"

Apparently, I didn't. But I was sure as hell ready to learn.

5

GOD, WHAT A DOUCHE BRADE DARBY TURNED OUT TO be. Not that I was surprised.

The firm had done some work the year before with a late-night talk show host. I didn't work on that client, and the people who did were not allowed to tell the rest of us who it was. But apparently, he was a total dickhead, too. I guessed that sort of thing was rampant among entertainers.

Lucky for me, most of the clients I dealt with were boring, old business people. Rich business people but still boring as hell. Which was fine. It kept the drama to a minimum.

But when I told Brade I'd been in a band in my college years, he looked at me differently. I guess that's why I told him—so he'd see me as more than a law firm stiff. Not sure why I cared other than I wanted to be one of the cool kids, too.

Of course, he had no idea how bad my band was. I mean, I went to a crummy little college in a crummy little town in West Virginia. It's not like there was much competition.

But he didn't need to know that.

I was quite sure, as he followed me to the door, that his eyes would have burned a hole in the back of my dress if he'd had anything to say about it. Thank god, I'd worn my Spanx.

And Brade the rocker wasn't so bad looking himself. He sort of had a Kurt Cobain thing going on with messy shoulder-length blond hair, a little facial scruff, and gray-ish eyes. He didn't smile a lot, but when he did, he had a dimple on one side of his face. Pretty damn cute, if you asked me.

Anyway, what a dumbass he was to assume I was a secretary. Although, that wasn't the first time. Wish I could have told him to kiss my ass. But in the world of working with clients, you kept thoughts like that to yourself.

Before he left, he gave me his cell number.

"We have a private show this week at a little place in Chelsea. Text me, and I'll leave your name at the door."

I glanced at his low-slung jeans, which showed off a very flat stomach framed by a huge rock-style belt buckle. My eyes wandered lower to further check things out…

"Oh, wow, that's really nice. Thank you." I doubted I'd take him up on the offer, but then a free concert was a free concert.

"And bring your husband. Or boyfriend," he said.

"Oh, I don't have—"

But before I could finish, he'd looked at me over his shoulder, winked, and was gone.

Shit.

I'd fallen for his trick. Now he knew I was single.

The question was, was he?

I WENT BACK to my desk, passing Eva's office. I was in luck. She was on the phone and had swiveled her chair away from the desk to face the floor-to-ceiling window. She was gesturing wildly, and through her closed door, I could hear her loud, animated voice. I rushed by before she turned around and saw me.

Sparkle had thoughtfully sent me a couple more matchmaking agencies to get in touch with. I looked them up on my computer, all the while with an eye on Eva's door. I never knew when she'd come flying out, ready to berate me for something.

"Thank you for calling the Tuscan Group," a voice crooned.

Sounded like a travel agency.

"Um, hi. My name is Maizy Strong—"

"Yes, Miss Strong?"

"Well, I wanted to talk to someone about your..." I looked around to make sure no one could hear me, "matchmaking services." I'd whispered the last few words when the guy from the mailroom came barreling through.

"Let me email you some forms to fill out, Miss Strong. As soon as you send them back with three photos—current photos, please—we'll get you set up in the database."

Sounded easy enough. "How long does it take to get dates?" Shit, that sounded bad. I hoped I hadn't disqualified myself by revealing too much desperation. But my review was coming like a freight train, and Eva never hesitated to hang it over my head.

"Well, that depends on you. How fast can you get your forms back to us?" God, she was cheerful. She probably had first pick of all the guys who came into the place. Kind of like working in a store, where you got to see the new merchandise before anybody else.

I craned my neck. Eva was still bitching somebody out. Probably her unfortunate husband.

"I can fill them out now." Why not?

"Super! I'll get them right over to you. As soon as we get you in the database, you'll start receiving emails about your matches."

Sounded so easy. What had I been waiting for? I should have done it ages ago.

"Oh, before you go," I said, "how much does all this cost?" I held my breath.

Please don't be too crazy.

"We have a couple different packages. If you sign up for an entire year, you get a twenty-five percent discount. If you go month-to-month, it's a bit more."

"How much more?"

Papers shuffled in the background. She had to look it up? Didn't they get questions like this all the time?

Maybe they based the price on how desperate they thought you were.

"It's one thousand dollars a month."

Huh?

She didn't say a thousand dollars, did she?

"I'm sorry. Could you repeat that?" I asked.

"Yes, of course. It's one thousand dollars a month. Unless you sign on for a full year."

Oh. I didn't have a year to wait.

She continued, "Along with the forms, I'll send over a credit card authorization form."

Of course. A thousand dollars for a few dates? I wasn't sure that even meeting the man of my dreams was worth a thousand dollars.

"Thank you, Miss Strong. I'll be on the lookout for your forms."

If she mentioned the forms one more time, I would have exploded.

"Spark, I don't know why you couldn't have worn something a bit more modest?" Our Uber driver tore across the city toward Chelsea, where we'd be catching Brade's show, blasting through almost every red light. I should have taken the bus. I'd rather get mugged than die in a Honda Accord.

Yes, I'd caved and texted Brade. How often was it one was offered VIP tickets to see a major rock star?

If you were me, never.

"Uh, Maiz, there is nothing wrong with how I'm dressed. I just like to show off a little." She sniffed and looked out the car window, the streetlamps flashing light, then dark, then light again on her annoyed face.

I don't know why I cared. Her halter-top was open nearly to her navel, but it wasn't my problem. If she bent forward, the girls would be out for the world to see.

Like I said, it wasn't my problem.

There was a line out in front of the club, but the driver dropped us where the velvet rope started. A huge bouncer—were there any bouncers who weren't huge?—was evaluating the breast sizes of the women waiting to get in.

We walked right up to him like we had the biggest tits in the city. Which, of course, we did not.

The moment of truth. Had Brade really left our names at the door? Or would we be humiliated and told to get at the end of the line like the average Joes we really were?

I'd be heading back home if that happened. No way was I waiting in line if we didn't get right in. In fact, I had my finger on the Uber app, ready to cut my losses and go home to a nice bubble bath.

But magically, the velvet ropes parted. We were in. I think it might have had something to do with Sparkle leaning forward and letting her boobs hang out, because bouncer guy didn't even look up our names on the list. In fact, I wasn't sure there even was a list. But who was I to look a gift horse in the mouth?

The club was dark and sexy, just like I knew it would be, with small groups of people in clusters of clubby-looking sofas and chairs. They were all amazingly good-looking and wearing the coolest clothes—the women wearing not much at all, and the guys in dark-wash jeans and T-shirts that looked like they'd been starched to within an inch of their lives.

Sparkle and I elbowed our way up to the bar, and she ordered us a couple fancy cocktails, because I guess that's what you did at a place like that. A beer or glass of wine would clearly have been way too common for people like us who'd been invited to party with celebs.

"Well, if it isn't my lawyer," a voice said from behind me.

Sparkle and I whipped around and there stood Brade in all his rocker glory—those sexy as hell low-slung jeans and a leather vest with no shirt underneath. His arms were covered in a crazy assortment of tattoos that I couldn't make out in the dim light, but his gray eyes and smile were front and center.

For me.

Okay, play it cool, girl. Heads were turning to stare at him, but the looky-loos were too cool to approach him. Which worked just perfect, for me.

"Brade!" I said, like I hung out with rock stars every day. I even leaned forward and did the air-kiss thing.

I got this shit.

My sister stuck her hand out, almost hitting me with it. I could swear she arched her back a little so her tits were more prominent.

More power to ya, girl.

"I'm Sparkle, Maizy's sister."

Holy shit, did her nipples just get hard? How did she do that?

When Brade extended his hand back, Sparkle pulled him into an air kiss just like I'd done. He air kissed her right back. Stars probably did that all the time.

He looked back at me, barely noticing Sparkle. Geez. *That* never happened.

"I'm not your lawyer, Brade," I said with a smile.

"Oh, right. Well, whatever you are, you're straightening out my legal matters. I appreciate that."

He really didn't need to thank me. I'm sure he was paying out the nose for my firm's services.

"You're very welcome, and thank you for inviting my sister and me."

"Always glad to have a couple beautiful women come see the show."

Just then a guy turned up next to him.

Shit, he had a twin?

"Ladies, this is my brother Penn."

I couldn't stop looking back and forth between the two. How was it the universe made two of the same perfect creatures?

Penn broke into a smile with a couple of the deepest dimples I'd ever seen. Brade had only gotten one, but it looked like his brother had cleaned up.

And Spark was a sucker for dimples.

"Nice to meet you both. Sisters, I guess?"

Sparkle giggled like a maniac. I'd have to talk to her about that later.

"Yup, we're sisters. I'm the fun one, and Maizy here is the brainy one," she announced.

Christ, why didn't she just say I was an ugly old maid virgin? What a shit. Heat crept up over my face, starting at my neck. My fingers crossed that in the dark, it would not be noticeable.

Note to self: kill sister later.

"Penn, I've never been to this club. Want to show me around a bit?" Sparkle asked in what I called her *fuck me* voice.

Bitch was deserting me. I'd get her later.

They wandered off, Sparkle's hand holding the crook of Penn's elbow. Wait 'til he found out she had a pet rat.

That left Brade and me. He pushed his fingers back through his hair and looked at the stage.

"Hey, I gotta finish setting up. Want to come backstage and hang out?" he asked.

Holy shit. *Um, yeah.*

"I'd love to. But before you turn around, there seems to be a fan behind you. A big fan. She looks like she wants to eat you," I whispered.

"Shit. That happens from time to time. Will you help me?"

Huh? "Um, yeah. I guess."

His lips were suddenly on mine, and damn if I didn't almost fall over from the thrill. He grasped the back of my head enough to let me feel his power, but not enough to make me feel like I couldn't tell him to go to hell.

I wasn't about to tell him to go to hell in case you were wondering.

He pulled back from our kiss—dammit—and pulled me to him with an arm tight around my shoulders. We started walking toward the stage, his gaze on the floor so he could politely ignore anyone looking at him.

So that was how they did it.

The wanna-be stalker stepped aside to let us part, still wearing her crazy-hungry look, and the others who'd noticed him continued to stare discreetly, quickly looking away when he got close.

Maybe he wasn't the douche I'd thought he was, and maybe I wasn't the boring-ass paralegal he thought I was.

6

CATO

I HATED MY JOB MORE THAN ANYTHING I'D EVER HATED. It was sucking the life out of me. Dreary work for law firm clients who got themselves in all sorts of ridiculous trouble. Day in and day out. Yeah, I got paid a shit-ton of money for what I did, but I'd never felt like such a useless human being in my life.

But no one knew that. I was the perfect employee and the perfect corporate suck-up. I deserved an award for my great acting. *No one* knew my true feelings.

Not even my one friend at work, Maizy. Beautiful, amazing Maizy.

Lots of people in the office thought they were my friends. I got invited to weddings, bar mitzvahs, and had even attended a few funerals. I went to their Super

Bowl parties, played on the softball team, and even did karaoke when the situation demanded it.

But I hated it all. And I didn't know how much longer I could keep it up.

"Hey, you ready for lunch?" Maizy asked, her head poking into my office.

She was goddamn stunning, as usual, with her hair in long blonde waves. She wore what she called her "work uniform"—a slim black dress, insanely high pointy black pumps, and a string of pearls. Even those goofy black glasses were gorgeous on her.

Yeah, I had a crush on Maizy.

Actually, I think I was even a little in love with her. But she didn't know it.

Like I said, I was one of the world's best actors. No one knew what went on in the *secret world of Cato*. And that's just how I liked it and planned to keep it.

"Yeah, let's go," I said, gladly leaving a boring-ass memo I was in the middle of for the senior partner I worked for. It was fine—I was ahead of schedule.

That was one of the reasons they loved me there at the firm. I was never late with any of my work, and it was always done to perfection. Little did they know how much I detested the long hours I spent there.

Anyway.

The one thing that helped me get through each week was lunch with Maizy. I looked forward to it all week long. Shit, I looked forward to it all weekend long. Sometimes, it was all I could think about. But I couldn't date anyone from work. It just wasn't done.

Not that she'd date me, anyway. You see, I was a former fat kid.

Now, I worked out five times a week. I was in great shape, actually had been since I realized in my freshman year of college that if I ever wanted a girl to give me the time of day, I needed to shed my baby fat and put on some muscle. So I started hanging out in the gym and learned about weights and so forth. Lost the weight pretty quickly. I wish I could say I never looked back.

Just because you're no longer a fat kid, it didn't mean you were a *recovered* fat kid.

See, you never leave that shit behind. At least, I didn't. No matter how fit I might look, I'd always be the chubby little asshole of my childhood.

That left me in the friendzone with Maizy, whose ass I was trying not to stare at as I followed her to the elevator.

"So, how'd your date go last weekend?" she asked, pressing *Lobby*.

Shit. Why did I tell her about that?

"About as you would expect it to."

She laughed. She loved my dating stories. I guess I loved the searing humiliation.

"Okay, give me some deets," she said.

"Well, the woman was...shall we say...*not as advertised*."

"Oh. That sounds bad."

"She was very nice." I hoped she'd let me leave it at that.

"Okay. We know that's a euphemism for something undesirable. You're not going to tell me what, though?" We pushed through our building's revolving door into the madhouse that was the typical New York sidewalk. We fell into the stream of people pouring in both directions and without any discussion between us, we knew where we were going. Same place we always had lunch. I thought of it as *our place*.

Maizy didn't know that, though. There was a lot she didn't know.

"Yeah. Okay. She went on and on about how her friends were all having babies," I said.

"Ohhhhh. One of those. I don't know why women don't just keep thoughts like those to themselves. They send guys running in the opposite direction. It's really not that hard to figure out."

We walked into our lunch place, a little diner owned by a Greek family, where they served the best comfort food you could imagine.

But to be honest, any place Maizy wanted to have lunch would be okay with me.

"You getting the regular?" she asked, looking through the menu.

As if either of us would ever deviate from the same thing we ordered every time we came. A BLT for me, and a cobb salad for her.

"So are you gonna call her again?"

Note to self: do not share date information with Maizy ever again. Too much mortification for one day.

She studied me. Thank god, she couldn't read my mind. She'd know that what I really wanted to do besides eat a BLT was pull up her skirt and—

Stop it, asshole.

"Nah," I said.

She leaned toward me on her elbows. "Well, I don't blame you. Manhattan is full of great women, and you have your pick of the lot."

Yeah, right.

"On a positive note…" I said.

Her face brightened.

"It looks like I'm getting promoted to partner. Senior partner."

Her mouth dropped open, and then she shrieked.

"Ohmygod, ohmygod, ohmygod!"

She had tears in her eyes. She was always on my side. Another reason I loved her.

I meant *like*. Another reason I liked her.

"You work so hard. You totally deserve it, Cato. We're going out for drinks to celebrate!"

That's what I liked to hear.

Except that we went out for drinks all the time. And that's all it was. Drinks.

"I'm so proud of you, Cato. You are really tearing it up at the firm." She leaned toward me. "Wouldn't it be great if someday you and I could work together? We could really run the place, couldn't we? We'd be so amazing. Although they say you shouldn't work with friends." She pursed her lips and gave me an *oh, well* look.

"Any word on *your* review? Eva given you any hints?"

"Ugh. She's so awful. I guess I haven't told you. She let me know that until I have a guy, like a fiancé or preferably a husband, that my opportunities at the firm will be, shall we say—limited."

"Holy shit, she can't say that." I hated that Maizy worked for such a bitch. The woman wasn't nice to anyone unless she wanted something, but she really rode Maizy.

"Yeah. At the party, she said that."

"She told you that at the firm party? Is that why you left so abruptly?" I asked.

Maizy shrugged while stabbing some lettuce with her fork. "Yeah. I was kind of freaked out. She basically said the wives didn't like their husbands working with a single woman. Like I was trying to seduce them all. They *wish*."

"Whoa. Sexism alive and well. A single professional woman is not to be trusted unless she's on the arm of a man. Holy shit. So what are you going to do?" I waved over the server for our check. I always paid because I made more money. Although I would have paid even if I didn't.

"Well, I guess Eva took pity on me because she invited me to a party at her house—"

"*Wait.* You went to Eva's *house*?" I couldn't even imagine that Eva had a house. She seemed like she flew around on a broom that never landed.

"I did. Isn't that weird? She invited me to introduce me to her brother-in-law."

Oh. Shit. Not good. I hoped he was a dick.

"He was pretty nice. Good-looking. Fun."

So much for that.

"But I don't think I could date a relative of my boss's. It's just weird." She shrugged. "I guess it was nice of her to try and fix me up, though."

Yeah, real nice.

We headed back to the office.

"So…I called a matchmaking agency."

Twist the knife a little, why don't you?

My heart sank back to where it usually was. "Really? What was it like?" I asked. Horrible, I hoped.

"I don't know just yet. I had to fill out this super-long online form. They asked just about anything you could think of. It was kind of weird. Supposedly, they'll start sending me guys to consider this afternoon." She turned to me as we entered the elevator. "Hey, maybe you can help me sort through them, if you have time."

Yeah, maybe I can pour acid in my eyeballs while I was at it.

"I only have thirty days until my review. Well,

twenty-eight at this point, if you want to be exact," she said.

"You've got to get a guy lined up before your review? Are you kidding?"

"Not kidding. But I think I can do it. There are plenty of nice people out there. I just have to make an effort. I need to put myself out there. It's not like they're just sitting under my nose, waiting."

Shit, she needed new glasses if she couldn't see what was right under her nose.

7

MAIZY

BACK AT MY DESK AFTER A NICE LUNCH WITH CATO, I opened my email to see if anything had come in from the matchmakers.

Nothing. Yet.

Nothing besides about twenty emails from Eva, no doubt ragging on me for being a less than perfect human being, employee, citizen of the Earth—you name it, and she'd find fault.

Thinking back to lunch, I had to admit I was a little thrown off by Cato's promotion. And now I felt like a shit. I mean, he was my friend. I should have been thrilled for him.

God, I was a bitch.

I knew he worked his ass off. All the senior partners

loved him. Rumor had it they even fought over who got to work with him.

So I should not be stung that he got promoted. For god's sake, he deserved it. I was happy for him, I was. But for some reason, it made me feel even worse about my own situation being stuck with a bitchy boss who thought I could do nothing right.

There was no doubt in my mind one of the reasons she thought I was such a lowlife was that I hadn't gone to an elite college. She was one of the many snobs at the firm, and let's face it, in the whole of New York City, who thought that unless you went to the best schools—the Ivies and a few others they deigned to acknowledge—you were a total dolt. Never mind that you could be smart as a whip or the hardest worker they'd ever seen. In her eyes, you were always less than.

But that was okay. I'd show her. Somehow, some way.

I was the first in my family to even go to college, much less graduate. My parents hadn't been what you would call the supportive types. They were just normal, middle-class people, working hard to pay the mortgage on our modest little house and to put food on the table for Sparkle and me. I never thought I'd done that badly. Until I moved to New York, that is.

I hadn't realized until then what real advantages were. Like parents who helped their kids with their homework. Hell, my parents never even asked about my schoolwork, much less got involved with it. Parents who sent their kids to educational summer camps. My family hadn't even known such things existed. And parents who encouraged after-school activities. I had to come right home and babysit Sparkle.

So in the end, I'd found myself at the mediocre local college. Considering where I'd started, I felt like I'd come a long way. But in the snobbery of New York, even that wasn't enough.

My phone pinged with the alert I'd set up for emails. Then it pinged again. Several more times.

I was getting emails from the matchmaker!

And lots of them!

I *knew* there were plenty of guys out there and that it was just a matter of getting in front of them.

I opened the first email from the agency. It included photos and a write-up on someone named Al.

Hmmm. Al looked like he was about sixty years old, even though his bio claimed he was thirty-one.

And it got worse. Al, catch that he was, went on to describe himself as someone who believed he should be the boss of the household…

I clicked the *no* checkbox and moved on.

The next guy looked better. In his photo, he was good-looking, wore a suit, and appeared to be about thirty-something.

Holy shit. He'd already been married and divorced three times. How do you even do that when you're only in your thirties? I had to give him credit for trying, though. He was definitely a marrying man. *Pass.*

It finally dawned on me why Cato acted a little weird when I asked him about *his* dates. The strange world of dating in the internet age was just a shit show.

I rang my sister.

"Spark, I don't know about the guys from the matchmaker. They don't look so good."

"Oh, c'mon. You're just being picky. There's probably a good one or two in there. You just gotta look," she said. "You know, Maiz, something looks off with Cher—"

"Oh, shit, here comes Eva." I hung up the phone in Sparkle's ear. She could tell me about her rat later.

"Maizy," Eva called, as if I weren't sitting five feet away from her.

"Hi, Eva. How's your day going?" Like I really wanted to know.

"It's going well. It could be better, though."

Here it comes.

"How could it be better, Eva?" I braced myself.

"Well, if you'd finished up that work I needed you to do for Braden Darby, my day would have been great."

What power I had, to ruin someone's day. Like I was god or something.

"Eva, I thought you needed my brief tomorrow." I could have sworn I had one more day.

"You know, Maizy, it wouldn't kill you to get something done early."

God, I wanted to kill her and be done with her passive-aggressive bullshit.

"If you'd like it today, I can finish it up for you right now." The damn thing was inches away from being complete. Why hadn't she told me she needed it sooner?

"Thank you. That would be good." She turned on her expensive designer heels and slithered back to her office.

I sighed deeply and rolled my eyes, just as she popped her head back in my cube.

Busted.

"I was wondering if you'd heard from my brother-in-law Anson?" she asked.

Ugh. I should have known that was coming.

"You know, Eva, he's super nice. But I don't know about dating one of your relatives. It seems so awkward."

"Well. Suit yourself. You know, it's not every day a guy like him comes along. Especially for a girl like you."

Oh, no, she did *not*.

She must have figured out from the look on my face that she'd stuck her big foot in her big mouth.

"Um. Excuse me?" I gripped the edge of my desk so she couldn't see my hands shaking.

"Oh, um, I meant that, you know, it can be hard for a woman your age to meet a nice guy. I mean, don't they say the chances of being struck by lightning are greater than meeting a single man—"

"I'm only twenty-eight, Eva."

"Right. Hey, I think I hear my phone ringing." She disappeared.

Jesus Christ.

Funny, though, that she'd asked me about Anson—he'd texted me only the day before.

Just like Brade.

I hadn't had time to get back to either of them. I wasn't sure I really wanted to, anyway.

I mean, date my boss's brother-in-law? Or a giant rock star?

They both sounded like accidents waiting to happen.

Just then, an IM from Cato popped up on my computer.

when we going for that drink?

anytime. tonight?

perfect.

Maybe I could discuss my dating dilemma with him.

Although...maybe I should keep that to myself.

Cato...Cato...Cato...

To be honest, Cato was handsome as hell. Tall, fit, dark hair and eyes.

He'd confided in me before that he used to be chubby. Or was it fat? He'd even showed me an old photo.

Never would have known it was the same guy. Chubby kid, glasses, acne.

Time and adulthood had been good to Cato, no doubt about it. Solid as a rock, nice slim waist, broad chest.

Not that I'd ever seen him in anything other than his work clothes.

But still.

Nah, he wouldn't be interested in me. He liked those young, skinny, model-types. Although, he never seemed to date any of them for very long.

I'd even wondered if he was gay. You never know.

Oh, what the hell was I thinking? I couldn't date Cato, a guy from work, just like I couldn't date my boss's brother-in-law or some musician.

I turned back to my matchmaker emails.

I like money, fast cars, and women.

You'll love my gun collection!

I'm here to meet one lucky lady.

Looking for someone who already has herpes.

God. Help. Me.

From under what rock did these cretins crawl?

I closed the matchmaking application and deleted every last email I'd gotten from them. I might not have had a ton of prospects, but I wasn't scraping the bottom of the barrel, either. Money, guns, luck, and herpes were not anything I was interested in, thankyouverymuch.

I was done. Playing it safe could go to hell. Anson, Brade, and Cato—even though he didn't yet know it—

were getting another look. They really *were* nice guys, and they seemed to like me okay.

I wasn't going to remain a middling paralegal for the rest of my days. No, now was the time to prove that I was a great benefit to the firm. I had a lot to offer, and they were going to start seeing it.

I wanted a damn promotion and of all things to hold me back, the lack of a boyfriend, fiancé, or husband was not going to be one of them.

My first step was to dial the matchmaking firm to tell them I wanted my goddamn thousand dollars back.

8

My last patient of the day was a rat. Named Cher. Yup, a male rate named Cher.

It was fun to treat a rat. I know that might sound strange, but my vet practice pretty much consisted of seeing dogs and cats all day. Anything other than that was a welcome change. I was always happy to see the odd snake, parakeet, or rodent. I wouldn't have minded seeing more of them to kind of mix things up, in fact.

"Hello, ladies," I said to the two attractive women who'd brought in the rat. They had to be sisters since they shared some similarities, but they sure were different from each other.

One, whose name was Sparkle—whose name is Sparkle, anyway?—was a hippy dippy chick with ruffled bell bottoms and braids piled on top of her head. The other one, Maizy, looked like she'd just come from an office uptown with her professional-woman clothes and big, horn-rimmed glasses.

"I'm Doctor Varten. What's going on with your little Cher?" My own dog—one of several— who had run of the place, was sniffing at the canvas bag holding the rat.

"Well…" Sparkle started to speak but her voice wavered and a big tear ran down her cheek. "I don't know, Doctor, but he's not eating much, and his eye seems runny."

Sparkle's sister put her arm around her and patted her shoulder.

"It's just that," Sparkle huffed, "I really believe he's my spirit animal. I have such an attachment to him. We meditate together."

Okayyy…

I looked at Maizy, who rolled her eyes.

All right. I got it.

One of them was a nut. The other was…well, I wasn't sure yet.

I mean, I felt for Sparkle, I really did. No one knew better than I did what it meant to love an animal. And what it meant to lose an animal. Hell, I became a vet because when I was growing up, we couldn't afford one. If one of our pets got sick, Dad would take them "out to the country." I was so determined to learn how to take care of animals, I'd gotten myself a part-time job at the local vet when I was just fifteen and stayed there until I finished college.

But meditating with a pet rat? I couldn't say I'd heard that one before. But if there's one thing you learn as a vet, it's that people have all sorts of relationships with their animals. And some of them were pretty out there.

"Well, let's take a look at Cher," I said, removing him from the small bag he was in. I picked up the little fella and realized Sparkle had been right. He was looking skinny, had runny eyes, and was barely moving.

"Can you help him, Doctor?" she wailed. Maizy hugged her tighter, and the dog tried desperately to lick him.

I rolled the lethargic rat over in my hands and listened to his heart and lungs with my tiny rodent stethoscope. I pressed on his abdomen to check for lumps or tumors, and he let out a sad little squeak. The tiny guy was sick, but he was going to live.

"Good news," I said, putting Cher back in his bag. "He has a respiratory infection typical of a rat. Some antibiotic drops will bring him around in a few days."

Sparkle sobbed. "Oh, thank god." She reached for a tissue and blew her nose. After a deep breath, she began to calm down.

Maizy looked from her sister to me. "Okay! It's nothing really bad. That's so great."

Sparkle sniffled loudly and nodded. "I...I know. I'm so relieved."

Wow. This Sparkle was one of a kind—some might

even say a little out there. Cute, but it was her sister who intrigued me.

A lot of women came through my practice. Not to say men didn't bring their pets in. It just seemed, more often than not, that the task fell to the woman of a household. And sometimes their pets were not really sick—I seemed to have attracted a small collection of groupies. That kind of irritated me because it took valuable time that I could spend on animals that really did need help.

"I don't mean to take too much of your time, Doctor Varten, but do you mind if I ask you some questions about caring for a pet rat?" Sparkle asked.

"Sure thing. Cher's my last patient of the day. Let's have a seat over here." The sisters followed me to a small table in the corner of the office.

While Sparkle lobbed a few rodent-related questions at me, her sister sat quietly, scrolling through her phone. When Sparkle stood to leave, her sister did, too. Her messy blonde hair and her heavy black glasses were a great combo.

"Your dog is so sweet," Sparkle said. The mutt had made himself at home, resting his big face on her leg.

"Thanks. I see a lot of animals that need homes, and I'm not good at turning any of them away."

"How many do you have?" Sparkle asked.

Ugh. This was always a bit embarrassing. I took a deep breath.

"Well, I have five dogs and two cats. One snake and one lizard."

Both sisters looked at me like I was out of my mind. I didn't blame them. You *had* to be out of your mind to take in so many animals, especially in the city. But when I saw a pet who was healthy and clearly had many happy years ahead of him, well, I wasn't going to let him be put down.

I walked them to the door. "So, Maizy, no pets for you?"

"Oh, no, Sparkle is enough to take care of." She laughed so hard her sister punched her arm.

I wanted to see this woman again, and if she had no pets to bring by my office, I had to cook up some other excuse. So I took my chance while Sparkle was tickling Cher inside the bag and the dog followed her like he was in love.

"Maizy, uh, I was wondering whether you'd like to get a drink with me some time?"

To say she looked surprised was an understatement. But I was okay with that. You had to put yourself out there, and I did just that on occasion.

She gave me a studied look, and I met her gaze head-on. She was free to turn me down—no harm, no foul. We were all adults.

"Sure."

"Sure?" I asked.

"Sure, I'd love to get a drink."

Well, then.

She jotted her number on a piece of paper she'd pulled from her purse. "Thank you. That would be fun," she said.

Sparkle continued talking into her bag as they headed out the door.

I finished the last of my paperwork while waiting for the night assistant to arrive, but I had trouble concentrating. Something about Maizy, and the quiet way she helped her distraught sister, had moved me. And it didn't hurt that she was drop-dead gorgeous.

The minute I got out to my SUV in the parking lot, I texted her.

u free tomorrow night?

To my delight, she texted right back.

tomorrow night would be great. meet at arnold's?

I loved a woman who knew what she wanted.

c u there

NEXT DAY, all I thought about was Maizy. Through the six cats I spayed and neutered, to the stray mutt I deloused, to the yellow lab that barfed all over my floor, Maizy—her blonde curls, big eyeglasses, long legs, and serious work look—was not far from my thoughts. I wasn't sure what it was about her, but I sure as hell was going to find out.

When I was done with my last animal, I zipped

home to get the animal smells off me with what must have been the world's fastest shower.

I walked into Arnold's, an old corner bar near China Town, and wouldn't you know, Maizy was already there at the bar with her nose in her phone. But when she saw me, the phone went right in her bag, and she lit up with a huge smile.

Yeah.

"Good to see you again," I said, settling into the barstool next to her.

"Likewise. Did you see a lot of patients today?"

I nodded. "I certainly did, but none as memorable as the rat named Cher."

She threw her head back with a delicious laugh. "Yeah, well. That's my sister. She's always been the eccentric one."

"And what about you?" I asked.

"What *about* me?"

"It sounds like you're the responsible sibling. You never do anything crazy."

She snapped her head back. "What? How would you know?"

Indignity had replaced her smile. I couldn't help it. I burst out laughing.

"You're cute when you're mad," I said.

"Ugh. Don't tell me that's your best line."

Sassy. Just how I liked it.

"Okay, then. Tell me the wildest thing you've ever done," I said.

She took a sip of her red wine, probably to stall for more time.

"I shoplifted some gum when I was in middle school." Satisfaction had replaced her indignity.

But I wasn't letting her off the hook.

"Maizy, every middle schooler I've ever known has tried shoplifting. I wouldn't put that in the wild category."

She tilted her head. "Okay, then. You tell me what you've done that was wild."

Fair enough.

"I rode a motorcycle across Thailand into Burma, where I was chased back out by some military thugs."

"You're making that up."

I held my hands up in the *I swear I'm telling the truth* gesture. "I really did do that. The summer after I finished vet school. I wanted to take a break before I started working. I wouldn't do it again. Being chased by thugs, with guns, in a foreign country is no fun. I do not recommend it."

Yeah. Top that.

"Well, there's a lot said for being the responsible sibling," she said defensively.

I'll say.

I reached for her hand. "You were really patient with your sister. That was very cool."

A drop-dead gorgeous woman, with a hippy sister named Sparkle, who had a rat named Cher.

I sure hadn't seen this coming.

THE PROMOTION

73

9

MAIZY

WHO WOULD HAVE KNOWN THAT WHEN I BROUGHT Sparkle and her rat to the vet, I'd end up having a drink with a handsome new guy just twenty-four hours later? Seemed like the gods of dating were smiling down on me, in spite of the disaster of the matchmaking agency.

But was I getting closer to having a significant other before my review?

Maybe, maybe not. But I sure as hell was exploring every option before me.

I'd been hanging out with some hot as hell men lately, but this guy just about put me over my edge. He had this tousled black hair and long-ish sideburns, some crazy thick eyelashes, and a slightly crooked nose.

Maybe from those thugs who chased him out of their country?

Who did that, anyway? Rode a motorcycle into a country where he didn't know the lay of the land. Before you went to a foreign country, didn't you check online to make sure it was a safe place?

I guess not everyone did that.

But I did. Or I would. If I were going somewhere. Which I wasn't.

"How'd you know you wanted to be a vet?" I asked.

He shrugged. He probably just fell into it. Guys did that.

I, on the other hand, had to beg and scrape for every little thing I got. And even then, it wasn't enough. On top of everything else, I was expected to be on the arm of a guy to really be complete.

Such bullshit.

"I always loved animals, wanted to help them. I liked science, so it was a natural path to follow."

I knew it. So much easier for men.

"What about you?" he asked.

"I'm a paralegal. It's kind of like a junior lawyer. I'm assigned a senior partner, and I do as much as possible with our clients and their cases until she needs to take it over."

"Ah. Must be so different from what I do. Animals coming in, you never know what you're going to get. And the owners can be even crazier than their pets."

"Kind of like my sister?" I asked with a smile.

He tilted his head. "Let's put it this way. I've seen more eccentric than your sister. But, this was the first time I had someone tell me they meditated with a rat." He laughed and shook his head.

The bartender dropped off another round of drinks, and Von took a deep draw on his beer. When he was done, there was a tiny bit of foam on his upper lip. I wouldn't have minded helping him out with that, using my lips.

Down girl.

Instead, I handed him a bar napkin.

"Oh, thanks," he said, dabbing at the spot on his lip that I'd pointed out.

"So do you ask out all the ladies who come in with pet rats?"

"Only the ones who have a very beautiful blonde, eye-glass-wearing sister." He swiveled on his barstool to face me.

Shit. My heart went thump.

Although I did think he was out of his mind for keeping so many pets. On the other hand, it spoke volumes that he cared enough about animals that he'd just take them in.

I glanced at my watch.

"Oh, geez. It's getting late," I said.

I sort of hated to leave. I loved the way this guy looked at me. Like he could see *inside* me or something. Wow.

"Yeah. I have to take the dogs for one more walk tonight." He waved the bartender over for the bill.

"This was fun, Von. I'm glad you took a chance and invited me out tonight." He really was something. So tall and handsome, good manners, funny.

He put his hand on my lower back as we worked our way through the crowded bar to the door.

"Thanks for joining me. I'd like to do it again," he said.

"I'd like that. Let's do it. I'll let you know how Cher makes out. Poor little thing. Who knew rats could have respiratory problems?"

"It's pretty common. In fact, it's how they often die in the wild when they don't have anyone to take them to a vet like me."

"I hadn't thought of that. Mother Nature's way of keeping the population in check, I guess."

"Exactly," he said.

He pulled open the door of my Uber ride, and I turned to wave as we pulled away from the curb.

I'd kind of hoped he might have kissed me. But if all went according to plan, there'd be time for that later.

WHEN I GOT HOME, I found Sparkle doing a handstand in the living room. Naked, of course. If she didn't care that people could see her through our windows, then I wasn't going to worry about it, either. And actually, since we were in New York and practically lived on top of our neighbors, I pretty much saw naked people out my windows all the time. Once you'd been in the city for some time, nobody seemed to care. It was like the constant blare of car horns. After a while, you didn't notice any more.

In fact, I'd actually gotten bored of spying on the hot gay guy across the way who cleaned house in his birthday suit.

"Hey, Sparkle."

She kicked her feet off the wall and landed on the floor, popping back into an upright stance.

"Hey, sis. Good day?" she asked.

"Actually, yeah. It was pretty good. Guess who I was just with?"

"Oh my god! You saw Brade?"

"No, I didn't see him. Although he texted me. I just had a drink with Von."

"Von? As in Von the vet?" She looked completely confused.

"That's the one. Von the vet."

"What? Are you kidding?" she asked. "When did he ask you out?"

"He got my number before we left his office. You were busy with the rat."

She put her hands on her hips. "The rat has a name, Maizy."

Oh, lord.

"Sorry. You were busy with Cher. I guess you weren't listening."

"Wow. You've got guys pounding your door down. That's freaking hot. I mean, sis, you've needed some action for a while," she said.

"Gee, thanks. But now there are too many of them."

"What? Are you kidding? How can someone have too many guys?" Her eyes were wide with disbelief. She often looked at me like that.

"Well, I can't go out with four guys."

She tilted her head at me as if I'd just said the stupidest thing in the world.

Had I?

"You can go out with whomever the hell you want, Maizy. Don't let that creepy boss at the law firm rain on your parade."

"Well, I don't know. I mean, I like them all. And they seem to like me. First, there's Anson, my boss's brother-in-law, who is hilarious and totally buff with his gorgeous red hair. He looks like that prince from England, Harry. Then there's Brade. You remember Brade, right? I believe you fucked his brother backstage at the concert they invited us to?"

"Yes, I remember him, and I remember his brother even better. In fact, we're going out this weekend." She looked very comfortable, sitting bare-assed on my sofa, with having been called out on having sex at a concert with a guy she'd just met. "So, who else we got? Keep running through your inventory."

"Right. Okay, well, we have Cato from work. Tall, serious, adorable. I've been friends with him for ages but I'm seeing him in a different light lately."

"Okay," Sparkle said. "Keep going."

"Last is Von. He's super-hot with his black hair and long eyelashes. And what's not to love about a vet? I mean, the guy can't say no to a stray dog."

Sparkle broke out in a smile. "Seems he can't say no to you, either."

"You're funny. Seriously, how am I going to choose?"

"What? Why do you think you have to choose? Go out with them all!" She rolled her eyes again.

"Oh, yeah, right. That'd go over great."

"No, Maizy. Date them all and see who you like. Sleep with them and see who's best in the sack."

"Ohmygod, you are crazy. I'm not a slut like you."

She settled back onto my cushy sofa. Still naked. Unfazed at having been called a slut.

"You might not be now. But there's hope for you yet."

THE NEXT DAY AT WORK, for some reason, Eva the bitch kept sticking her head in my cube. God, that woman killed me. I mean, one minute she was destroying me with her slow, relentless torture, and the next, she acted like we were best friends.

You couldn't be friends with your boss.

But that didn't mean they have to be your enemy, either—did it?

After about her tenth drive-by, she revealed her true intentions. She was probably getting a sore neck from craning it so hard.

"Hey," she started, like she was some kind of normal person. "Guess you're seeing my brother-in-law tonight, huh?"

Well, shit. Note to self: remind Anson to NOT tell her anything else about me. It was weird enough I was going out with a relative of my boss.

I shuffled some papers on my desk, hoping she'd leave. But she did not.

"Um, yeah, Eva. I'm seeing Anson tonight."

She stood there, silent. Clearly waiting for me to say more.

I wasn't going to, though.

"Okay, then." Good lord, she was surrendering. "I'm sure you'll have a very nice time. You know, Maizy, I usually only introduce him to the highest quality women. But I thought—"

Was she bringing that up again? Insufferable was what she was. And I was about done taking her shit. I could be like that. Calm, cool, collected, but when you go a smidgeon too far—well, all bets were off.

"Eva, it sounds as if you feel I'm beneath your

brother-in-law, and that you're doing me a favor by introducing us. If you really do believe I'm such a bottom-dweller, maybe I should call him and cancel." I reached for my phone.

"No!" She waved her hands frantically. I'd never seen her do that. "You misunderstood me."

I gave her the most polite stink-eye I would muster.

Her composure returned. "Like I said, I'm sure you'll have a nice evening." She gracefully turned on her heel and headed back to her office.

That's right, bitch.

10

ANSON

DAMN IF MY SISTER-IN-LAW HADN'T BEEN ALL OVER ME to call her paralegal, Maizy, for a date. I mean, I had every intention of calling. I thought she was a cool woman, very nice-looking, and I wanted to hang out with her. But Christ, it wasn't like I was sixteen years old when I had to be prodded to talk to girls.

I didn't know how my brother put up with her. I also didn't know why he married her, to be honest.

I'd grabbed a cab from my office in the financial district over to the art gallery party where I was to meet Maizy. I'd offered to come by her office and pick her up, but truth be told, I was relieved as hell when she said no. I don't think either of us wanted to run into Eva when we were together. She'd find some way to make it creepy and weird.

I was really looking forward to seeing the lovely Maizy. It wasn't every day I met someone as hot as her, with that wavy blonde hair and long, long legs. And she was smart, to boot.

For a moment—just a split second, really—I'd entertained *not* calling her just to spite my sister-in-law. But how stupid would that be? Talk about cutting off your nose to spite your face.

I walked into the gallery and immediately spotted my buddy Scott, the owner.

"Hey, bro. How's it going?" he asked, giving me his usual bear hug.

"I'm well, dude." I looked around the gallery. It was full of something he called *neo-modern*. If you asked me, it was all weird as shit, but I kept my mouth shut when it came to art. He knew what he was doing, no doubt. In less than one hour, the place would be full of buyers, and by the end of the night, he'd be nearly if not completely sold out. I'd bought a couple paintings he'd insisted I purchase. I wasn't thrilled with them, but I had to admit, when I'd gotten them home and hung them, they'd done wonders for my bachelor apartment.

"So, I believe we'll see some very beautiful women here tonight, my friend," Scott said. He might have had strange taste in art, but he had great taste in women.

"Ah. I actually have someone joining me here tonight."

He rolled his eyes. "Not another fix-up by your sister-in-law, is it?"

Oh, that's right. He'd heard about the last one.

"Actually, this one I did meet through my sister-in-law. But this girl is cool. You'll see."

The door buzzed behind us, and Maizy walked in, taking my goddamn breath away. Scott sucked in his breath, also in appreciation.

She had enough hair for two people, and the masses of it tumbled down her shoulders in waves I was dying to run my hands through. Maybe I'd get the chance to, later.

She was wearing high-heeled fuck me shoes and this tight little red dress that flared out just above her knees.

And the glasses. Of course, she had the glasses. After she spotted me from across the room, she pushed them up on her head and made her way over to us.

"Holy shit," Scott whispered before she got to us.

"Anson!" she said, throwing her arms around me.

I could get to liking that.

"Maizy, this is my friend Scott. He's the owner of the gallery and our host tonight."

"Great place," she said, looking around. "I've walked past here many times and always wanted to come in."

Scott could barely take his eyes off her. "Well, it's about time we had you visit, isn't it? Enjoy your evening, and let me know if you have any questions about the artwork. I need to take care of my intro-verted artist over there before he has a panic attack." He scooted off.

"Can I get you a drink?" I asked Maizy.

"Yes, please. After the day I had…"

I grabbed her a glass of white wine from a passing waiter.

"Don't tell me," I said, taking a swig of my beer. "Your boss getting under your skin?"

She rolled her eyes. God, I could feel her pain.

She looked down at the floor, slowly shaking her head, as if she was holding something in. Which I guess she was because she exhaled this big blast of air.

She started to speak and stopped. Then she started again.

"How does your poor brother tolerate that woman?" She looked relieved, having expelled the negative thought.

"I know. I wonder the same thing. I have no idea. He was a nice, normal guy until she pussy-whipped him."

She shook it out of her head. "Ugh. Let's not let her ruin our evening."

"Cheers to that," I said, clinking my beer bottle against her wine. "Let's grab a seat over here."

Not only did Scott know how to pick out art that sold like hotcakes, he'd also done up his gallery like it was a little nightclub—with the lights on full-blast so you could admire (and buy) the artwork, of course. I led Maizy to an intimate little seating area where we sank into a cushy sofa. She watched the people coming in, walking around, checking out the artwork.

I, on the other hand, watched *her*. Discreetly, of course. Didn't want to be a creep about it.

"Do you ever buy any art from Scott? He has some really cool stuff here," she said.

"I have bought a couple pieces that he picked out for me. I don't know a thing about art. I couldn't tell you whether they're good or bad. But they do look nice in my apartment."

She swiveled on the sofa until she faced me. "Thank you for inviting me tonight. This is awesome." She shimmied her shoulders a bit. Like a happy cat, purring.

"I'm glad you were free. And may I say, you are stunning tonight?"

She looked down at her wine while a faint pink blush washed over her face. I loved that she was modest.

"Thank you. So you work in the financial district?"

"Yup. Over by Wall Street. Yup, I'm a finance guy like nearly every other asshole here in New York."

She threw her head back and laughed.

"Well, do you like it?" she asked.

I had to think about how to answer that one.

"It's okay, I guess. I took over my dad's small firm when he retired."

"No kidding. A family business," she said, her gaze searching mine.

"Thank you. Yeah, I'd been working at the firm

since college, so it only made sense. My mom really wanted me to carry it on."

"Where are your parents?" she asked.

"Out on Long Island. I really don't see them enough. I feel crappy about it."

"Does your brother go out there often?"

"He does. He makes up for my being a bad son." I wasn't really a bad son. I think I just said that for sympathy. I stood and pulled Maizy to her feet. "Let's take a walk around."

I'd helped Scott build out the place, so I knew it like the back of my hand. In fact, a couple years prior, when the heat went out in my apartment in the middle of winter, I slept in the gallery for a few days. It worked out great.

"I just love this painting," she said, pointing at something that looked like a pot of paint had been spilled on it.

"Um, yeah. It's really cool."

I caught her looking at me. "You don't like it at all, do you?" She was wearing a huge grin.

Busted.

I wasn't a very good liar.

I looked around to make sure no one could hear, and shrugged. "I don't get it. I mean, what the hell is it?"

She was going to think I was a total dick now.

Instead, she put her hand on my arm.

"It's cool. Everyone has their own tastes." She

looked around at the paintings. "I can totally see how these might not appeal to everyone."

At that, I needed to kiss her. There was no way I was waiting any longer. I leaned toward her, and she fell right into me. So I kissed her harder, finally having the opportunity to sink my paws into that gorgeous blonde hair. There were a few people milling around us, but shit, I didn't care. It was a freaking art gallery with weird-ass paintings all over the place. A public kiss was no big deal.

I pulled back, pressing my forehead to hers. Her eyes slowly fluttered open, and her warm breath washed over me, a combination of something minty and white wine-ish. I kept a fistful of her hair in my hand, amazed at its silkiness. I wanted to take things further and bury my face in it, but I knew to go slow.

Girls like Maizy were worth waiting for.

11

MAIZY

Holy cow, was Anson a good kisser.

That, coupled with the delicious white wine, and the heady gallery atmosphere, left me swaying on my feet. I knew if I didn't get a wall or something to lean up against soon, I'd be down on my ass.

"Hey, can we sit somewhere? I'm really warm," I said.

"'Course, beautiful." He led me by the hand toward a non-descript door. "Wow. I've never made someone pass out before. Maybe I shouldn't let you sit down. Fainting women are sort of a bucket list kind of thing for me."

Good sense of humor? Check.

We passed through the door into an office that looked like an extension of the cozy seating areas in the main gallery. There were fluffy white sofas and love seats and even an easy chair with a huge ottoman. An iMac sat on a rustic-looking desk with a couple neat piles of paper, and just above it was a huge window that looked out into the gallery. I peered through it to the party on the other side, which was quickly filling up.

"That window, my dear, is a one-way mirror," Anson told me.

"What do you mean? It doesn't look like a mirror to me."

"It's a mirror on the other side. That means we can see out but no one can see in," he explained.

Oh, my.

I plopped my butt on the edge of the desk as my dizziness faded, and Anson moved right in for the kill, pressing me against the hard wood. I was pretty sure I felt his growing erection against my leg, even though he seemed to be sort of trying to hide it.

His lips were back on mine, and he smelled like expensive, spicy soap. I laced my fingers through his thick, red hair and parted my lips for some sexy exploration.

It was funny, but a newfound excitement had my heart racing in both a rush of emotions and reservations about kissing my boss's brother-in-law, not to mention having gone on a date with Von just the night before. But I pushed that out of my mind.

There'd be plenty of time to fret over that later.

Anson pulled back, his gaze piercing mine with some kind of crazy, stony power that sent a warm throbbing to the center of my core. I glanced out the window that I was sitting just inches from and saw the party in full swing.

"It's kind of hot, isn't it?" he asked.

"What? What is hot?"

He nodded toward the glass just behind me. "You know. You know what I mean. Don't pretend you don't."

Ugh. Busted. I totally knew what he meant. He was right. And he looked at me so intensely, he might as well have been seeing right through me.

"Here, baby," he said, taking my hand and guiding me off the desk and back onto my feet. "Face the window. With your hands on it."

I did as he said.

"Now, get closer."

I scooted up to the glass until I could see my breath on it, and he stood behind me, whispering in my ear.

"See all those people? Just milling about, looking at art, maybe thinking about buying something. Do you think they're wondering what's going on on the other side of the mirror facing them?"

"I...I don't know," I muttered.

"I think they are. And they have no idea we're standing right here. They have no idea how turned on you are. And they have no idea that I'm about to unzip the back of your dress."

Shit. If I wasn't leaning against the window, I might have toppled right over.

His fingers breezed down my back. Cool air tickled my uncovered skin as he pushed my dress down my shoulders and to the floor. I stood in my bra, panties, and high heels, separated from the rest of the party by only a piece of glass. And a rising passion that was bordering on explosive.

Pushing my hair aside, Anson ran kisses down the side of my neck while unclasping my bra. As soon as that fell to the floor, his hands were on my breasts, kneading as he pushed me against the window, my head turned so my cheek lay on it.

"Are…are you sure no one can see us?" I murmured.

"Yeah, baby."

Unable to hide it any longer, his hard cock ground into me. I pushed my ass back to increase the friction on his dick, and a growl sounded in my ear.

"You're so hot, Maizy. And your tits feel so good."

He whipped me around until I faced him, his lips crushing against mine again while he reached inside my panties. I exploded in goose bumps with my back pressed against the cool glass, but his touch had set a fire burning between my thighs. Before he went any further, he checked in.

"You good, baby?"

"Yeah," I said, thrusting my hips toward him to let him know just how good I was.

His fingers burrowed into my wet pussy, sliding up

and down my lips and spreading my wetness from my clit to my ass and back.

"God, that feels so nice," I managed to whisper.

"Take my cock. Please," he said.

I'd already begun unbuttoning his shirt. When I reached his belt, I opened his pants and through a tangle of trousers, shirttails, and boxers, I grasped an erection that I couldn't fit my fingers around. I dug deeply until I got to the root of his cock, and as my fingers wandered down to his balls, he sucked in his breath.

"Fuck, baby, that feels so good. Keep going. Work it," he demanded while he continued stroking my own heated sex.

I could feel my orgasm build as he ran his thick fingers against my clit, into my pussy, and back. And it was clear from his trembling, as he pressed me against the window, that his own explosion was coming.

"Oh, god, I'm coming," I managed to mumble as my head banged back against the glass. I knew the folks in the gallery couldn't see me, but they must have heard my moans.

And I didn't give a damn.

Just as I was at the peak of my orgasm, Anson's cock erupted in my hand with thick streams of hot semen. We pumped each other until our shaking legs would no longer hold us up and staggered over to the office's sofa, me naked except for my panties and heels, and him dragging his pants and boxers around his feet, trying not to trip.

Quite a look.

Actually, it was really funny. I tried not to laugh, watching him do an odd walk with his still-hard cock bouncing around, but a little giggle turned into a torrent of laughter, and when he looked down, he, too, began to roar.

"Hey, everybody okay in there?" a voice yelled. The doorknob jiggled but it was locked from the inside. Thank god.

"Shit," I said, standing and moving as fast as I could to retrieve my clothes. Someone was going to come flying in, and I was nearly naked. I clutched my dress just in case they did.

"Yeah, Scott, it's us. We'll be right out," Anson called.

"Oh, okay, bro. I was thinking that was you in there," Scott said, his footsteps fading as he walked away.

"If he was thinking it was us, why'd he come knocking?" Anson whispered as he tucked himself back into his pants. He pulled a monogrammed handkerchief out of his pocket for me to wipe off my hands.

I smoothed down my dress as he zipped me back into it. When we were in one piece again, we returned to the party wearing big smiles on our faces. No one noticed a thing.

But the painting I'd been admiring?

Gone.

Dammit.

"Spark, wake up." I shook my sister, who pushed her eye mask up on her head and looked around, confused.

Her eyes darted around the room, settling on me. She looked me up and down in a panic. "What's wrong? Oh my god, Maiz, what's wrong?"

Maybe I shouldn't have woken her.

Too bad.

"Spark, I just had the most fun date with Anson, the guy my boss introduced me to!"

"You woke me up for *that*?"

"What? This is important. Besides, you wake me up all the time. Like to show me that new trick your rat could do."

"That's different," she moaned, pushing herself up in bed and pulling the covers over her—you guessed it—naked body. "Whatever. Tell me what happened."

"We went to his friend's gallery for a really cool show. Great artwork." I traced my finger over Sparkle's bedspread.

"What? C'mon, spill it."

"Well, we messed around a little."

She clapped me on the back so hard, I almost fell off the bed. "Awesome! You got some nook-nook. I'm proud of you, big sister."

Well, she didn't have to put it like *that*.

"Do you like him?" she asked.

I nodded. "Yeah. I think so. Even if he is related to my boss."

"By marriage, for heaven's sake," she said.

"Yeah. I do feel a little skanky, though. Von last night and Brade tomorrow night."

She yawned loudly. "I'm going back to sleep now. You're a big girl. You'll figure it out." She yanked her eye mask back down over her face and burrowed under the covers.

"Goodnight!" she sang.

That was my signal to leave. And yes, it *had* been a good night.

BRADEN

It was pretty cool that Maizy was taking care of my case and that we were becoming friends. I mean, it was hard to believe I was spending time with anyone in the legal profession, but this girl was cool as shit. She'd been in a band, after all.

And I was dying to know if she could sing. So I was taking her to karaoke. I had my hair tucked up into a cap and wore some tinted aviator-style glasses in the hopes that no one would recognize me. Sometimes I seriously missed my anonymity.

I had a driver for the night so we didn't have to bother with cabs and such, and when we pulled up in front of her building, she was waiting out front on the stoop with her sister Sparkle.

"Hey, pretty ladies," I called out the car window. I popped out, gave Sparkle a kiss on the cheek, and Maizy one on her sweet lips.

"Sparkle, you wanna join us?" I asked.

"Oh, that's so nice, thank you. But I have a yoga class to teach tonight. You kids go have fun. Don't get into any trouble," she called over her shoulder as she ran up the steps to her door.

Maizy looked at me with that killer freaking smile. "That was nice of you, Brade, to include my sister."

"Well, the more the merrier, right?" I guided her to the car, and we hopped into the back.

She swiveled on her seat to face me. "So. Where're we going?"

"I told you it would be a surprise. And it will be."

"Aw, c'mon."

"Patience, my pretty," I said, grabbing her fingers and bringing them to my lips.

Her hand fit mine like it was made for me, and when she gripped me back, I knew I wouldn't be letting go anytime soon.

Was I turning into a pussy, or what?

The driver pulled up before a non-descript building. No one was around but a burly bouncer standing next to a door that looked like it opened only from the inside.

I knew better, though. I'd heard about the place and had wanted to check it out for a long time. My touring schedule kept me from doing a lot of things I liked, but I was in town and taking advantage of the free time.

"What is this place?" she asked, looking around nervously.

I kissed her cheek and smiled.

As we approached the door, the bouncer stepped aside and by some sleight of hand, managed to open it. We entered a small place wildly lit with black and neon lights, a long bar, and several tables with chairs. On a small stage directly ahead was a dude with a white-knuckled grip on a microphone trying to sing the Police song *Roxanne*.

Eh, I shouldn't bust on someone for not being a great singer. Most people weren't. And I had to give a shit ton of credit to anyone who got up on stage. Even when you were a professional like me, it was hard, much less when you were just messing around with your buds.

"A karaoke bar!" Maizy exclaimed, looking around. "I've never been to one."

"I thought it would be fun, and one of the guys in the band told me this place was awesome. Kind of off the beaten path, on the exclusive side."

"Ha. Who knew karaoke could be exclusive." She laughed. "But don't you think everyone will know who you are when you get up on stage?"

I led her to a table and waved over the server. "*I'm not going to sing. You are.*"

Her eyes about bugged out of her head. "What? Me? Why?"

"You used to be in a band. I want to hear you sing," I explained. And, I wanted to see her gorgeous ass up on stage.

"Well. I don't know. It's been a long time."

I took her hand again. Damn, it felt good.

"If you don't want to do it, you don't have to. But I was hoping you'd give it a try," I said.

"Yeah. Maybe." She pursed her lips. "I gotta think about what I want to sing."

Her face brightened. "I know just the song. You'll have to wait and see. I'm not telling you," she said with a wicked smile. She got up to approach the disc jockey and after a bit of negotiation, she pranced back to the table to wait her turn, her blonde hair bouncing.

It would seem I'd made a good call.

"There are four people ahead of me," she said.

"Cool. Hey, I understand your sister is going out with my brother Penn."

"I know. It's cute, isn't it? I suppose at some point, we four could all go out together," she said.

"I suppose. But I already spend a ton of time with my brother. He only recently moved out of my place into his own."

"Is he part of the band? I mean, does he tour with you?" she asked.

"Most of the time, yes. He helps the roadies, the

managers, and so on. We've been together so long, I can't imagine it any other way."

Family talk. The "sads," as I called them were sneaking around, threatening to swallow me up like they sometimes did.

But now was not the time. I was with Maizy, and I wanted to know her better. In a variety of different ways.

"Were you close growing up?" she asked.

"Pretty close. I mean, he's five years younger. But when my dad died, I had to take him in."

"Wow. Sorry to hear you lost your dad. But Penn seems like a great guy."

I looked down into my beer. "Yeah, he is. And he's forgiven me."

"For what?" she asked.

Oh. She didn't know. I thought everyone knew about the low point of my life.

"I was driving and got into an accident. Penn and I made it." Christ, I still choked up when I talked about it.

She studied me with those gorgeous eyes.

"Oh. I'm so sorry."

"Thanks. Yeah. Dad didn't make it. My fault."

"Maizy, you're up," the DJ called, scanning the room for my girl.

Shit, did I just say *my girl*?

She squeezed my hand and stood, running for the

stage like a damn rock star in her sexy skinny jeans and high-heeled boots. She took the mic from the previous singer and smiled, looking around the room.

She was a freaking natural.

The music started, and I instantly recognized the song. Shit, *I'd* sung that song before.

Imagine by John Lennon.

You've got to love a girl who likes John Lennon.

She closed her eyes and took a breath before she belted out the first line. And holy shit, did she nail it.

Would it have been weird if I just proposed to her? Right there in that bar?

Because I was tempted.

As she hit all her notes with near-perfection, I was spellbound. It wasn't every day you came across a beautiful, smart woman who could freaking *sing*.

She swayed through the song, closing her eyes during the chorus, and I swear I got a bit choked up.

I was definitely turning into a big ol' pussy.

On her way back to the table, the DJ stopped her, probably to tell her what a great job she'd done. She was all smiles. There was nothing like owning a song, something I knew all too well.

"Holy shit, you were awesome!" I said.

"Really? No, you're pulling my leg."

I loved her modesty.

"Did you notice the room got completely quiet when you were singing? That never happens in karaoke."

"Oh, I guess so. It was fun." She took a swig of her beer, still grinning from ear to ear.

"Why'd you drop the band you were in?"

She shrugged. "I don't know. I mean, we weren't going anywhere, and I was interested in a career in law."

"I see. How do you like it there at the firm?"

"I like it. Most of the time. I mean, the work is interesting and challenging. Most of our clients are pretty nice. My boss is a bit of a problem, though."

"Oh, right, what's-her-name. The lead attorney on my case. Crabness?"

"Crabtree. Eva Crabtree. She's pretty much a bitch on wheels. One minute, she's nice, and the next, she insults you. And she's been hanging a promotion over my head—"

She stopped short.

"Yeah? What about it?" I asked.

"Oh, nothing," she said, shaking her head.

Hmmm. What was that all about?

"Hey, you want to hit the road?" I asked. "I don't have anything going on tomorrow but I think you might have to go to work."

She took a quick look at her watch. "Ugh. You had to remind me," she said, shaking her head.

"Well, the car's out front. We can go anywhere we want." I knew where *I* wanted to go. But I was a patient man.

I paid the check.

"You're very beautiful, you know," I said as we settled into the car's backseat.

She looked down. "Thank you."

I hooked a finger under her chin to bring her mouth to mine. Her lips were everything I thought they'd be—soft, warm, delicious, and full of possibility.

13

MAIZY

Karaoke! Now that was a surprise.

What wasn't a surprise were all the women in the bar—and some men—who stared at Brade. And he was completely oblivious to it. A few even started to approach our table, but I scared them off with my bitch face.

Again, he took no notice.

I hated for the evening to end. Brade was great company, not to mention handsome as hell, but I had to work the next morning, and honestly, I was a bit tired from my date at the gallery with Anson the night before. And Von the night before that.

Dates three nights in a row. With three very exceptional men. Wasn't I the little hussy?

But I wasn't going to worry about that just then. I

was in the backseat of a limo, in Brade's arms, and it was pretty freaking breathtaking. And, he'd shared a very personal story with me.

At first, his kiss was soft, but the second I parted my lips, he pressed against mine with a passion that took my breath away. Like he was dying of thirst and I was his glass of water. There was something about him that was so familiar and comfortable, even though we'd really only just met. When I thought about it, it was weird to be with a rock star, but when I looked at him as just a normal guy, there was nothing out of the ordinary.

He pushed a button that raised a dark window between us and the limo driver. I wasn't sure what he had up his sleeve, but I couldn't wait to find out. In fact, I found myself in the mood to take over. So, I did.

I pushed him back in his seat and straddled him, one leg on either side of his hips. His eyes were partway closed, and I could feel his dick harden through his blue jeans. He groaned quietly as he pushed his hips up, grinding his erection into me.

With my lips on his and our tongues exploring, his hands flew under my shirt and up to my breasts. He kneaded and pulled until I wanted to scream.

Oh, what the hell.

I peeled off my top and threw it on the seat beside us. Next went my bra, giving him full access. I had to admit, limo sex had always been a dirty fantasy of mine. If I didn't go for it then, who knew when I'd have another chance?

"God, you have great tits, Maizy," he murmured, his lips moving to them. He took one in each hand and gently pulling them together, burrowed into them. The sensation sent a bolt of need right through to my core, which was starting to throb in a massive way inside my jeans.

"I've never had sex in a limo," I confessed to him in between kisses.

He pulled back and met my gaze with a smoldering look. "It sounds like you might like to."

"I kind of would," I admitted, beginning to open his pants to free the hard-on I'd been grinding on.

I lifted myself off him to shed my boots and jeans. Reaching into a pocket, he produced a condom before lowering his pants beneath his ass. I climbed back on top of him and while he sheathed himself with the rubber, I played with my clit, hanging heavy and sensitive. His fingers gently pried open my pussy, and he ran the head of his cock up and down my slit, spreading my moisture.

I was wild with need. All I could think about was being full of this man's cock. I wanted to be closer to him, as close as I possibly could.

"Are you ready, baby?" he asked.

"Yeah. I want you to fuck me," I whispered.

Shit, I was a dirty girl.

He groaned and pointed his cock right at my opening, where he entered me an inch or so, giving me a moment to adjust to his girth. When he was fully seated inside me, after taking his time, I ground down to take him deeper, as if that were possible. The sensation of being full of him was almost too much. I began to piston on him wildly, desperate to come.

"Hey, hey," he said. "Slow down, baby. I don't wanna come too fast." He placed his hands on either side of my hips to try to control me, but it didn't work.

"Oh, god, I'm coming…" My head bucked, banging against the roof of the car, as I fucked him. His hands encircled my waist, and he thrust up inside me one more time. He growled like an animal through his orgasm, pumping me until he ran dry.

"Shit, baby, you're incredible. Come home with me tonight, please."

I was exhausted, and the thought of spending the night with Brade sounded heavenly. In fact, I couldn't wait and dozed off in the car before we even got there.

THE NEXT MORNING, Brade had his limo take me home. The driver waited while I changed for work and then delivered me to the office. What a sweet deal. I could get used to being driven around town in a car that was always waiting for me wherever I went.

And don't you know, I ran smack into Eva in the

elevator. There were too many people around to really have any sort of conversation, but the minute we got off on our floor, she started the grilling I knew I was in for.

"Have a good time with Anson?" she asked, as if she and I made small talk all the time.

Yeah, you nosy witch. I had a good time with Anson. He's fucking hot as hell. And I had a great time with Von and Brade, too…

But she didn't need to know any of that.

"It was very nice," I said with the blandest smile I could muster. I was hoping that would be the end of the conversation.

"Oh, good. I had my husband call him to find out, but he wouldn't provide us any information."

I knew I liked that guy.

"Yup. Good stuff," I said, continuing to smile like an idiot. "Oh, shoot, I have a call in two minutes. Gotta run," I lied as I zipped off down the hall.

When I got to my cube, there was a wrapped package sitting on my chair. What the hell?

It was the size of a tabloid newspaper and very light in weight. I tore off the package's plain brown wrapping and gasped.

Holy shit.

It was the painting I'd admired at the gallery a couple nights before.

I read the enclosed card to find Anson had *bought me the painting.*

I couldn't believe it. Not only was it about the most thoughtful thing anyone had ever done for me, but it was also incredibly generous. I sank into my chair with the painting in my lap, shaking.

Somebody bought me a painting.

My mind immediately flew to where I would hang it in my apartment when I heard footsteps outside my cubicle. I quickly tucked the painting under my desk before anyone saw it and started asking questions.

A lump formed in my throat. Anson, Von, and Brade were terrific, and I was about to test-drive Cato. I might never get my promotion, but I sure was spending time with some high-quality men.

I sure as hell couldn't knock that.

14

CATO

Was I actually, finally, going out on a date with Maizy?

Holy shit.

It was about freaking time. I'd had the hots for her since we met on her first day a few years before. The senior partner I worked for caught me checking her out and had taken me aside.

"Cato, my friend. I see you admiring our new paralegal—the blonde."

He'd busted me and had gone on about "not dipping one's pen in the company inkwell," and all that. He said he'd seen disastrous things happen when a rising star at the firm (did he mean me?) got involved with someone at the office, etcetera, etcetera.

I got the message, loud and clear. I would remain

firmly in the friendzone with Maizy 'til the end of my days. Or until she or I left the firm.

Then, I could pounce.

But as the weeks and months went by, and we became closer and closer, no one else I dated even came close to her. I mean, she was beautiful, sure. But also smart as a whip and kind, to boot, with the way she helped her somewhat crazy sister.

So, I'd run out of patience. Exhausted all other options. I'd dated like a maniac, not hard to do in Manhattan, which is teeming with single people looking to hook up. But there were few women I wanted to see a second time, and none I wanted to see a third time. I was clear on what I wanted, and I was done with the friendzone. The opinions of the senior partners could go to hell.

So when my boss, Steve, was headed to Europe for two weeks with his family and gave me access to his kick-ass penthouse apartment on the Upper East Side, I figured it was time to make my move.

I mean, the place came with a goddamn cook.

Yeah, the senior partners at my firm did *that* well. They had penthouses, cooks, and went to Europe for their kids' spring breaks.

I was on that track, I supposed. All I had to do was play my cards right.

Which I wasn't going to do.

I swung by Maizy's desk to check in.

"Hey, Maiz. What do you say to heading out in an hour or so?" I asked in a low voice.

She looked past me to ensure her bitch boss was not in earshot. She was also moving around something under her desk, but I couldn't make out what.

"Yeah. Sounds good." She looked around again. She was *so* not sneaky. But I liked that about her.

"You sure it's okay? Hanging out at Steve's?" she asked.

No, it probably wasn't okay. But he'd never know.

"'Course it's okay. He gave me his keys. Wait 'til you see the place." I'd been over to Steve's many times, along with the firm's other attorneys, but he didn't lower himself to socialize with paralegals. Another thing I hated about the firm.

Not an hour later, we headed out in my car. Yeah, I drove to work. They gave me a parking space, so why the hell not? I sometimes gave Maizy a lift home so she didn't have to take the subway. But more often than not, I was at the office until nine p.m. She was usually long gone by then.

I glanced over at her scrolling through her iPhone while I navigated the horrendous rush hour traffic in my Volkswagen Golf. The people at the firm gave me shit for driving a car like that, but I couldn't have cared less. They could take their BMWs and Teslas and shove 'em.

"Just checking in with Sparkle," she said. "Wanted to let her know where I'd be."

"How is the sparkling Sparkle?" I'd met her a few times, and let me just say that woman was a piece of work.

Maizy laughed. "She's fine. Dating a new guy. They seem to like each other. At least they *sound* like they like each other. The other night, they were at it in her bedroom until they finally conked out at around two a.m." She shook her head.

"Oh, shit. I forgot about the joys of having a roommate." And boy, was I glad those days were behind me.

I pulled up to the garage at Steve's building and after flashing the card he'd given me, pulled right into his spot.

What a life, to have a permanent parking spot in Manhattan. It was what I aspired to.

Not really.

But street parking, which was what I had when not at work, did pretty much suck. First, it could be a bitch to come by, and second, car break-ins were endemic. I practically had the place that fixed broken car windows on speed dial.

We grabbed the elevator that went straight to Steve's apartment using the security key he'd given me.

"Good lord, they have a private elevator?" Maizy asked.

"Yeah. Can you believe it? Wait 'til you see the place."

The elevator doors opened, and I got a whiff of

what promised to be an incredible dinner, thanks to the cook he left behind to feed me. Maizy gasped.

"Oh. My. God. Look at this place," she said, walking in and doing a three-sixty degree turn.

"Yeah. Lawyering has been good to Steve," I said, looking around with her.

Two walls' worth of windows provided expansive views of Lower Manhattan, and the other walls were covered in what I was sure was very expensive artwork. Maizy was drawn right to it.

"Check this out," she said, craning her neck to see more.

"You can walk around. No one's here except the cook. I'm gonna check in with her. You feel free to roam."

"Okay," she said, wandering down a marble-tiled hallway.

"Hello, Mr. Cato," the cook, Mel, said.

"Hi there. Smells great," I said, heading over to the stove to get a look at our feast.

"Dinner will be ready in half an hour, Mr. Cato. Can I bring you and your friend some drinks?"

"That'd be great, thank you. Um, I'll have a scotch, and she'll have some champagne."

I settled into a cushy sofa in the living room while I waited for Maizy to return from her snooping. Mel dropped off our drinks just as Maizy made her way back. God, I loved watching her walk through that gorgeous apartment.

"This place is out of control," she said, continuing to look around. "Just, wow."

She settled into the sofa next to me. "Oooh, bubbly. Thank you."

"So, Eva still ragging on you?" I asked.

She rolled her eyes. "Of course. She wouldn't be Eva if she wasn't."

"Right. Right."

Go ahead. Ask her.

"So, um, what happened with her brother-in-law?"

There. I'd done it.

But maybe I shouldn't have. Maizy's face went from pink to bright red in a second. She looked down at the bubbles rising in her champagne flute.

"He's nice. Yeah. Nice guy." She nodded.

Okayyy, we won't talk about that then. But it was funny because she usually didn't mind telling me about her dates.

Things were different now. At last.

"How 'bout you? Any more online adventures?" she asked.

"Nope. They haven't worked out that well for me." I shrugged.

"And what about your promotion? Are you totally psyched? Will you be getting a penthouse like this?" She threw her head back and laughed, one of my favorite sounds.

"I don't think I'll be getting anything like this, anytime soon. Don't think I'd want it, anyway. And I'm not sure I'm all that excited about the promotion, either." I hadn't shared this with a soul.

Here come the questions.

Her brow furrowed. "What? Are you serious?"

We moved over to the dining table, where Mel was serving.

Oh, what the hell. I didn't have to pretend with Maizy. "To be honest, I don't really like the work I do. Never have. In fact, I kind of hate it."

Her eyes widened. "You're kidding. Is this a joke? I thought you loved your work."

"Everyone thinks I love it. That's how I got promoted, I guess." I sliced into what must have been the most perfect filet mignon I'd ever had. I could get used to Steve's life. No doubt about it. But I probably never would.

"Wow. I had no idea. I'm so sorry. I never knew," she said.

Her compassion got me. Right in the gut. Not that I expected any less. It was what I loved about her.

Oh, shit. I said love.

Whatever. It felt damn good to share my big secret with her.

I looked at the ice cube melting in my scotch, creating blurry streaks in the amber liquid. "I've hated it for a long time," I confessed. And boy, did it feel good to get it off my chest. "I just haven't been sure what to do about it."

"What would you rather do, work-wise?"

"Maybe something in nonprofit. I'm just not really liking law."

She looked at me like I had two heads. "I'm astounded. You never said anything. Not a thing." She took a sip of her champagne. The way she was looking at me just then…well, something was different.

I was getting the distinct feeling that the friendzone might at some point be a thing of the past for me.

15

MAIZY

WHAT A FREAKING PALACE CATO'S BOSS STEVE LIVED IN. I was just blown away by the views, the marble floors, and the outright fanciness. No wonder people became lawyers. And no wonder it was so cutthroat at the firm. Everyone wanted to live like Cato's boss.

But I had to say, not even *my* boss lived quite like this. 'Course she wasn't one of the founders of the firm, and she hadn't been around as long as Steve had. But she was still doing okay. I'd been to her house, after all.

Damn. Cato wanted out of the law firm. I never would have guessed that, not in a million years. He'd always seemed to love his work. But I had to say…it made me like him even more, that he had other interests and wasn't driven entirely by the money. I could totally see him working in nonprofit, maybe running some sort of agency, or even being their in-house counsel. He wouldn't get paid the same, but he had simple tastes. He'd do just fine.

And maybe even be happier. Nothing wrong with that.

We'd finished up a cooked-to-perfection filet mignon served to us by Steve's cook—how many people had someone freaking cook for them?—who was now laying out some kind of homemade ice cream thing with espresso coffee poured over the top. It had an Italian name I would never remember, but it was beyond delicious.

"So what are you going to do about Eva's mandate?" Cato asked.

Hmmm. How much to tell him…?

"I don't know. What would you do if you were me?" I asked.

Ha. Deflection.

He sat back in his dining chair, head tilted while he studied me.

"I have an idea," he said.

I wasn't sure why, but my heart started to thump. And the room grew warm.

"What's that?" I asked.

"Well, you could date *me*," he said matter-of-factly, as someone might announce rain was coming.

And there it was. The elephant in the room.

When you're friends with someone for years, have lunch and drinks every week, cry on each other's shoulders about dating and such, it seemed as though something like this was bound to happen—a growing affection. How could it not?

Because it sure was for me. And it looked like it might be for Cato.

"You think I should date you, do you?" I asked, my voice shaking.

He shrugged. "Yup. You would if you were smart, anyway."

Whoa. He was going for it.

"Well, I guess we're gonna find out if I'm smart."

Why not have a little fun?

"Look," he said, "I know you have another guy you're dating. Actually, maybe even more than one. I'd like you for myself, but I am patient. But if you're going to date around, I think you should give me a chance, along with anyone else you're seeing."

He walked over to my side of the table and reached for my hand. I stood and followed him to the sofa, where our evening had started. Somewhere along the line, Mel had lit a fire in the living room fireplace. The room was toasty, and after the bubbly, I didn't have a care in the world. No job crap, no sister crap, and best of all, no dating crap. I was relaxed and ready for a good time as I sank into the plushy sofa.

I reached for his hand.

"I think that is a fair request, Mr. Cato Lowell." God, I wanted to kiss him so badly just then. So I figured I would. No time like the present, and all that…

I leaned toward him, and he tilted back for a split second, not something a girl wants to see when she's trying to be gutsy. While I tried to figure out what to do next, he must have screwed up his own courage, because before I knew it, I was enjoying his mouth on mine.

Bingo.

God, he felt good. I wanted him to drink me until there was nothing left. There was something so magical—and comforting—about falling for someone you trusted so much and knew so well.

Never mind that I'd been with the other guys just before. But it didn't matter. I wouldn't let it. Cato's touch was fresh and new. Really, all of them were so totally different and yet so completely magical. Special. Beautiful.

God, I wished I could have them all.

But in what kind of world does that happen? And when all was said and done, who knew if any of them would want *me*, anyway?

I could end up alone, with no promotion, and still distrusted by folks at the firm who thought I was a single floozy.

Exactly where I'd started.

But for now, I relished Cato's fingers in my hair as he clenched a handful every now and then as if to ensure it was real—and that the moment itself was real. And I found myself searching for his assurances as he searched for mine, running my fingers through his hair in return, like he might go away at any moment.

He pulled back and looked at me sternly.

"You know how long I've wanted to do this?" he asked.

He'd wanted to do this for a while? He'd wanted to kiss me?

No complaints here.

"No. I never knew. And by the way, we work together," I pointed out. Not that I wanted anything to stop. I just thought I should call out the obvious.

But he didn't seem worried about a thing as his lips brushed over mine, then across to my ear and up my temple, where he stopped. His breath was light and warm on my skin.

My eyes fluttered closed. I didn't want the moment to end.

He pulled me to standing. Holding one of my hands, he bent to remove my shoes. When he straightened back up again, he was several inches taller than I— taller than I ever remembered him being, I guess because I always wore heels when I was around him. He then began to work the buttons of my silk blouse, so very slowly, his gaze catching mine to ensure I was okay with his advances.

Hell, yeah, I was okay with him removing any and all of my clothing.

When my blouse was open, he untucked it from my skirt and tossed it to the sofa behind me, stopping to admire my nude lace bra and the nice cleavage it gave me. Reaching around, he unzipped my pencil skirt, pushing it down over my hips until it fell to the floor at my feet.

Taking a small step back, he looked me over from head to toe as I stood there in my bra and panties.

"Beautiful," he murmured. "Beautiful, just like I knew you'd be."

Good lord. If he kept talking like that, I might just have to marry the man.

"C'mon," he said, leading me toward the bedrooms.

We entered a sumptuous room that reeked of expensive, well, everything. Some talented interior designer had decorated it with richly textured fabrics in amazing, unexpected colors. It smelled of the old, crackled leather on the chairs in the corner that over-looked the city. But most breathtaking was the unob-structed view of Central Park and beyond. Cato lowered the lights in the bedroom so we could see better out the windows.

He walked up behind me, his hands falling on my shoulders. He pushed aside my hair, his lips traveling down my neck. His touch was soft but strong at the same time, left a trail of fire on my skin and a throb between my legs. I had to feel his lips again on mine, and I spun around to face him.

"I'm so glad you invited me tonight," I whispered.

"Thank you for joining me. You don't know how many times I've thought about this."

God. How many hints had I missed? What an idiot I was.

I went for the buttons on his shirt and pushed the starched fabric back over his shoulders. He might have been a fat kid at one time, but those days were long past. I brought my lips to his broad shoulders and ran them over his beautifully defined pecs. He smelled like a dream—spicy deodorant mixed with a long day of hard work. Oh, if I could bottle that, I'd be a rich lady.

As I ran my kisses up his neck to his ear and back to his mouth, my hands flew to his belt buckle where I made quick work of his pants and boxers. They thudded to the floor in a puddle at his feet, and he released me long enough to remove his shoes and then the rest of his clothes. He stood before me, and before the window overlooking the best part of Manhattan, fantastically nude, his now fully-erect cock bouncing against my stomach as my mouth returned to his.

Was I flying? Because it sure felt like it.

My Cato. My dear, dear Cato. What had taken us so long?

Because I couldn't help myself, I felt for his erection, and when my hand landed on it, he gasped loudly.

"Do you have a condom?" I murmured into his ear.

This might have been our first date, but I had to have this man inside me or I was going to lose my mind. To hell with respectability. It would seem I didn't have any, anyway.

"Yeah, baby," he said, leading me to the bed. He

reached for his trousers on the floor and after rummaging through a pocket, produced one that he tore open and rolled down his hard length in one smooth movement.

He lay me back on the bed and reached to unhook my bra. He slid my panties off after I kicked my shoes aside, and we were both naked together for the first time after being friends for years. Something about it was so precious, I found I had a lump in my throat, which I quickly swallowed away. I could be mushy later.

He looked over my nakedness, slightly shaking his head like he couldn't believe what he saw. He parted my legs and climbed up on the bed between them.

"Are you ready for me, beautiful?" he asked.

Oh, hell, yeah.

I couldn't speak, so I just nodded. He was so striking in the dim room, which was lit only by the glow of the city lights. I could make out shapes and angles, but the details were indistinct. It all added to my exhilaration.

He hovered over me, the warmth of his body whispering across my skin. He got closer, so close that he pressed against my dripping core and lay his forehead against mine in such an intimate gesture, I wished he could just swallow me. Swallow me whole.

I felt myself open as he pushed, entering me a scant inch. I drew my breath, and he pushed further. I couldn't help but roll my head back and forth in ecstasy and in anticipation of more.

Oh, my god, I was with Cato. Cato, my darling, sweet work friend. And now, lover.

His mouth landed on the side of my neck while he held himself up with one hand, the other kneading my breast as he drove himself inside me, deeply, all the way.

I screamed. I couldn't help it.

He pumped me fast, sliding in and out like lush silk. I was immediately in heaven. The sensitive nerve endings in my core drove lightning through my entire body, where it exploded out of my every pore.

His lips brushed mine one more time before his moans filled the bedroom. I felt like all of Manhattan could hear us coming, and I didn't care. I wanted everyone to know how our coming together was complete and total magic. I was awestruck. This was a man I'd get to see every day. Well, at least Monday through Friday.

16

VON

"STANLEY! GET IN THE CAR!" I YELLED TO MY BLACK LAB. Out of all the dogs I had, this one was just out of his puppy stage, and for some reason, was taking longer than usual to train. I worked with the little bugger day in and day out, and he was still the naughtiest dog I'd ever had.

I rotated which dog I took to work every day, and the ones left at home were taken out by the dog walker. It really boosted their socialization to come to the office and be around people and other animals, although they were kept out of the examination area—I couldn't have them catching anything from other sick animals.

Stanley finally tore himself away from whatever stinky thing he was smelling and hopped into the backseat of the car when I started the engine. He was smart enough to know that meant his ride was leaving, and if he wanted dinner and a warm place to sleep, that he'd better get with the program.

So he clearly wasn't dumb. Just hard-headed.

All day I'd been looking forward to my dinner that night with Maizy. In fact, I'd been looking forward to it since the day she'd come in with her kooky sister and rat named Cher. Beautiful, together women were hard as hell to come by, and I didn't want to let this one slip through my fingers if I had anything to say about it.

I got home and put Stanley out on the terrace to play with the other dogs. That way, they'd be out of the way while I was making dinner. I wanted to put on a nice spread—tasty, but not too fancy—so I planned to make the spaghetti and meatballs dinner my mom had taught me. It was pretty much always a crowd pleaser.

I knew she'd like my apartment, too. When my parents had passed away, they left me a small chunk of change, which I'd turned into a down payment on a pretty nice New York apartment. It wasn't a palace by any stretch of the imagination, but it had two levels with access to a huge rooftop terrace. Not bad for a vet from Smalltown, USA. My only regret was that my parents had not lived to see it, nor how successful my vet practice had become.

The only thing missing in my life? A nice woman to share it with.

Sure, there were tons of women in New York. And I

had plenty of dates. Just not very many who I wanted to see a second time. And even fewer who I wanted to see a third or fourth time. Actually, there were pretty much *none* who I wanted to see a fourth time, now that I thought about it. I don't think I'd had a fourth date with the same woman since I'd been in veterinary school.

Maizy was different, though. I mean, of course I didn't know her very well. Actually, I didn't know her at all, if I were to be honest about it. But the minute I saw her, something jolted me. I know it's totally cliché, but it truly was like someone was standing behind me, pushing me toward her. Like maybe my mom or dad were watching and wanted to let me know not to let this one slip through my fingers. Something similar had happened to me before, mostly just when I saw a hot girl whom I wouldn't have minded seeing naked. But I wanted way more than that with Maizy. Her sexy braininess grabbed me and hadn't let go since I'd first seen her.

How is it that a girl like that is even single?

Or *was* she single? She'd agreed to have dinner with me at my place. You didn't do that if you had a boyfriend. Right?

My sauce was on the stove, bubbling gently, when she rang and I buzzed her in. I popped open a nice Chianti Classico and poured two glasses while I waited for her to come up in the elevator.

When I pulled my door open, I don't think I was

ever so glad to see someone. The second she walked in, I felt like I could breathe for the first time in years. Jesus. What was it about her?

"Hey," she said, planting a kiss on my cheek and giving me one of her dazzling smiles.

Her hair was piled on top of her head in one of those messy knot-things, and she had a little smudge of makeup under her eye. It all contributed to making her even more gorgeous. I thought to tell her about the errant mascara or whatever it was, but it was so cute, I wanted to look at it for a while longer. She was perfect in her imperfection.

I handed her a glass of Chianti and watched her check out my kitchen. Her tight blue jeans and high-heeled boots caused a twitching inside my boxers and a rush of blood through my veins.

I knew I liked her, but shit, I didn't know I liked her *that much*.

"Cheers," I said, as we clinked glasses.

"Great place," she said. "It's just amazing."

The dogs, curious as hell that there was a stranger in the house, pressed their noses against the sliding glass door from where they were banished on the terrace.

"Thanks. I'm really fortunate to have this place. When my parents passed, and I sold their farm, I ended up with enough for a nice down payment." I followed her gaze past my living room, complete with an operating fireplace, and back to the modern kitchen I'd had installed. "I'd never dreamed I could end up in some-place like this." It was absolutely true. Veterinarians do well, but not *this* well.

"Good lord. You really do have five dogs, don't you?" she asked, smiling and watching them jump all over each other.

I laughed. "Yup. It's impossible to turn them away when you know they're going to end up in a shelter." It was a serious weakness of mine. But not a bad one to have, if you asked me. "Not only do I have a whole pack, I've gotten nearly everyone I know to take in one or two strays. Maybe you can take a couple, see how they get along with Cher the rat."

She scrunched her face. "Pretty sure that's not allowed in my apartment building. In fact, I don't think we're even allowed to have the rat, but it came with Sparkle, and there was really nothing I could do about it. At least it's in a cage unlike the rest of the rats in New York City."

"Cheers to that." I took a swig of my wine. "Rats are actually great pets. Low maintenance, and they stay pretty healthy."

"Sounds like the perfect boyfriend," she said, throwing her head back and laughing.

Damn.

"Speaking of which," I said, "do you have a boyfriend?" I felt a quick *thump* in my chest. God, I was becoming a pussy.

She shook her head. "No. I do not."

But something in her face said there was more than just a "no" answer to that question. I wasn't going to push it, though. Whatever it was would come out later. If there was going to be a later. Which I really hoped there would be.

I served my sauce over some nice, fat bucatini pasta.

"Oh, my god. This is amazing," she said with small moans of appreciation.

Of course, the twitching in my dick was now on high alert.

Down boy.

After dinner, she helped me clear the table. "Hey, I have to take the dogs for a walk," I said.

"Okay. Let's go."

I opened the door to the terrace and five happy pups barged into the apartment and straight for her.

"Easy, guys," I said, trying to pull them off her. But she was unfazed by the paw prints and drool they left all over her blue jeans.

Gotta love that in a girl.

When I'd leashed them all up, I corralled them, and her, into the elevator. We wandered across the street to Central Park. She shivered, so I handed her the dogs and properly zipped her jacket right up to her chin. A couple raindrops landed on her pretty face.

"Oh, shit, rain. I gotta walk the dogs, though. Do you want to wait inside?" I asked.

She shook her head, and some of the hair that had

fallen out of its clasp floated around her face. "No, I'm coming with you."

Well, I don't know if lightning struck me just then, but something did. Even the dogs sensed it. They sat patiently, looking up at both of us.

So I leaned in for a kiss and to my delight, she leaned right back toward me.

17

MAIZY

GOOD LORD, IF VON HADN'T KISSED ME JUST THEN IN
the park, in the rain, I may have just had to attack him.

But thank goodness he finally did, and damn, was it
worth the wait. His lips brushed mine at first, as if in a
test, and then they parted, allowing him to tickle me
with his tongue. The guy left me breathless. Seriously,
why had he waited so long?

Anyway.

With the dog leashes in one of my hands—the little
buggers had gone completely silent as they stared up at
us—I moved my other to his chest, a rock-hard promi-
nence of muscle and hard-earned strength. The guy
clearly didn't spend all his time at his vet practice. And
when I brushed over his nipples, I could have sworn I
heard him suck in his breath.

Ah. I'd discovered his soft spot. Well, at least one of them.

We might have been in the middle of a chilly path in Central Park, but the heat inside me exploded like an out of control wild fire. The rain came down harder, trickling into our lips and mouths. Instead of being an annoyance, it only served to heighten the growing throb between my legs. Time stood still as I got lost in Von's kiss. I wanted to stay lost there.

But of course, life doesn't work that way. One of the dogs, soaked and most likely getting cold—and still having to pee—began to whimper. Another quickly followed, and pretty soon all five of them were asking if we couldn't please cool our jets and get a move on. *Who did we think we were anyway?* they seemed to ask.

Panting, I pulled back from Von. The rain, having plastered his hair to his head, trickled down his face in rivulets. The dogs were equally as soggy, although they didn't look nearly as happy about it.

"C'mon," he said, taking my hand and pulling the dogs over to a grassy patch where they could relieve them-selves. As they proceeded to sniff, as dogs did, to find the perfect spot, Von ran his hand over my matted hair and wiped a raindrop on the end of my nose with his thumb.

The dogs were gathered back at our feet, presumably done with their business.

"Let's hit it," he said.

We started to run back to his building, the rain

pelting our faces and the dogs trotting behind us. All I could do was laugh. How lucky was I to be running in the rain with this gorgeous man and his assortment of mutts, like I didn't have a care in the world?

We got inside his building and shook ourselves off just like the dogs did, leaving little puddles of water on the lobby floor and the elevator.

"Wait here just a sec," he said when we reached his front door. He removed his shoes and disappeared into his apartment, returning with several towels.

"Do you mind?" he asked, bending to towel off his fur babies.

Of course I didn't mind warming up the shivering pups. We both knelt in the hallway and rubbed all the water we could off their fur, and then let them inside where they crammed into a couple dog beds by the radiator. Von took my dripping jacket, shaking it off on the tiled floor like it was no big deal. He tilted his head in a *follow me* fashion. Which, of course, I did.

Aside from the kitchen, I'd not seen much of the place, so I was glad to crane my neck and snoop while I followed him down a long hallway and into a bathroom.

A bathroom?

But I wasn't confused for long. He pushed my hair back over my shoulders and slowly lifted my shirt over my head. He then reached for the fly of my jeans, making quick work of that. I kicked off my boots so my jeans would fit over my feet, and as soon as I stood there in my black bra and panties.

He was down to his skivvies in no time and reached into a huge, tiled shower stall to turn the water on full blast. As steam filled the room, he bent to kiss me again while he reached around my back to unfasten my bra.

"I've wanted to touch you since the first day I met you. Actually, I wanted to do more than that. A lot more," he whispered.

"Oh, yeah? Like what? What more do you want to do with me?" I teased.

He stepped back, and with a very serious expression, ran his gaze over me from top to bottom.

"For starters, I might remove those panties," he said.

"But they're the only thing I'm wearing."

"Yes. That's the point."

"Well, what about yours?"

I pointed at his boxers, now with a huge tent in the front, courtesy of what I guessed was a nice-sized erection.

He followed my gaze, hooked his thumbs in the waistband of his boxers, and swept them to the floor where he kicked them aside.

Holy shit.

Now that I could appreciate all of him, I took a moment to take in the perfect splay of hair across his chest that narrowed into a thin line leading directly to more hair, and of course, his huge, bouncing erection.

Who knew the friendly neighborhood vet—or

should I say, rat healer—was sprung from such god-like genes?

So I returned the favor and dropped my own panties to the floor. His gaze wandered over me like warm honey. I pressed my legs together, hopefully discreetly, so he wouldn't see the moisture dripping from my core. I had a feeling he'd know how wet I was in a few short moments.

Taking my hand, he led me into the steaming shower, and we both stood under the sharp spray, any lingering chill from the rain quickly disappearing down the drain.

I leaned my head back into the spray to rinse out my tangled hair. Von's lips flew to my neck, and his hands to my breasts, where he ran his fingers over my slippery skin before finding my hard nipples. My hand found his cock, now bouncing hard against me. Wet from the shower water, I stroked him until I could swear he got even bigger. He moaned loudly, his eyes fluttering closed while his head lolled back.

"Hold on, baby. You're gonna make me come," he said, gently moving my hand. He reached for a bottle of shampoo and squeezed a small amount into his hand.

"Turn around," he demanded.

Now behind me, he began massaging the most amazing-smelling shampoo into my hair. He lathered it up on my scalp like a pro and somehow knew to let just a little of it dribble down to the long ends. Maybe he'd washed some other woman's hair in his past? I didn't know, and I certainly didn't care. His fingertips massaged my scalp until I thought I might pass out. It was a good thing I was close to the shower wall, because I wasn't sure my shaking legs would support me.

Of course, I barely knew this guy, but I was so drawn to him. Not only was he gorgeous and built like a Greek statue, he also had a soft spot for animals and could cook a pasta sauce like nobody's business.

What wasn't to love?

Once he'd worked up a fantastic lather, he turned me back around to make sure that while he rinsed my hair, nothing ended up in my eyes. I felt like a goddess, being attended to by deft but sweet hands.

Good grief. How did I get so lucky?

And now it was his turn to get lucky.

I grabbed the bar of soap and worked up a lather in my hands.

"Now you turn around."

I soaped up his back, running my nails over the surface of his skin. As first, he tensed from the sensation, but then relaxed into it, leaning onto the shower wall in front of him, resting his head on his hands.

I directed the shower spray to rinse him and then lathered my hands again. This time, I reached around his hips for his hard-on and stroked him with my slippery fingers.

"Oh, Christ," he murmured, pushing himself into my hands for more.

I rested my head on his muscled back. "You like it, baby?" I whispered.

"Fuck, yeah. Stroke me like that. I'll come in your hand," he growled.

I ran my other hand over his hard chest while I pumped him faster. He drove himself balls-deep into my hand one last time, and he moaned as warm streams of cum spurted into my hand and onto the shower floor.

"Jesus, baby," he said, slowly turning back to me. He held my wrinkled hands under the water to rinse them, then stepped underneath to rinse himself. He shut off the shower and opened the door, steam filling the bathroom. He helped me step out of the stall, reaching for a fluffy towel that he wrapped around me, and one for his own waist. What a sight. The guy had just come, and already had another erection.

Good lord was I in trouble. First, Anson, then Brade, then Cato.

And now, Von.

THE NEXT DAY at work I was fairly floating through my meetings and work, that is, until Eva popped by my cube and burst my bubble. I came crashing back to earth and braced myself for her dig.

"Maizy," she said simply.

Oh, god. What the hell was she up to?

I smiled brightly, clenching my fists under my desk. "Eva! How's your day going?"

She placed a cheek of her skinny little ass on the corner of my desk, pushing the papers I was working with onto the floor.

And no, she didn't pick them up.

"Fine, Maizy, my day is just fine."

Then what the hell did she want?

"I wanted to remind you that review time is about two weeks away now. I was wondering if you'd given any thought to what we discussed at the firm party?" she asked.

I'd given plenty of thought to her being the biggest bitch on wheels. But I didn't think that's what she was asking about.

So I played dumb just to mess with her.

"What do you mean, Eva?" I asked, my smile still bright.

"Well, you know, about what you need to do to really excel at the firm."

"Oh. Like find a husband? Is that what you mean, Eva?"

Ha. I had her. She looked like she wanted to crawl out of her skin.

"Well, that's not *exactly* what I said, Maizy. But how are you progressing in that area?"

"Yeah, Eva, I think we both know someone doesn't

find a guy, get engaged, and then get married in four weeks flat."

Is it possible she hadn't considered that? I'd thought she was smart. "Right. Right. I just wanted to know if you'd made any progress. Like with my brother-in-law."

"If what you're asking is whether I'll be married to your brother-in-law in two weeks' time, I'd have to say the answer is *no*."

"Right. Of course."

I should have just turned her lame ass into human resources. But I didn't want to ruin my career. At least, not yet.

Her office phone rang, and she jumped up to run for it.

That's right, bitch. You'd better run.

But she had gotten me thinking, and I did need to do something about the guys and I had an idea. I just had to see if they'd all go for it.

18

ANSON

I GUESS THERE WAS A FIRST FOR EVERYTHING.

I was headed over to Braden Darby's house to meet him and another guy Maizy was supposedly dating. The Maizy I'd gone out with just a few nights previous.

I know, right?

What the fuck?

When she'd invited me over, I thought it was one of the freaking strangest requests I'd ever heard.

But I was a big believer in shaking things up. So I said *yes*.

On top of that, I couldn't believe I was going over Braden Darby's house. I didn't even know he lived in Manhattan. And on top of that, he and Maizy were dating?

I had to admit that, in spite of my puzzlement with

the entire situation, I was psyched to meet him. And of course, to see Maizy.

I didn't blame Maizy for playing the field. She had a lot going for her.

The beautiful, sexy, Maizy.

She was amazed by the painting I'd surprised her with, which thrilled me to no end. As soon as I'd spotted her checking it out, I mentioned to my gallery buddy to set it aside. Yeah, he'd given me shit for being pussy whipped, but hell, he was always thrilled to see art go to a happy home. And to make his commission, of course.

And most importantly, Maizy was pleased as punch.

My Uber ride dropped me in front of a massive brownstone row house. Damn, I'd thought I was doing pretty well for myself thanks to the world of finance, but it would seem being a rocker was far more lucrative. Well, good for him. I remember when Braden's band was nothing, playing college campuses and crappy little bars. I'd been following them way back then. He'd worked his ass off and now played Madison Square Garden and huge arenas like that.

A heavy wooden door swung open when I rang the bell. "You must be Anson," Braden said. There he was, in the flesh. A little taller and thinner than I'd expected.

"Hey," I said, extending my hand. "I already know who you are. Good to meet you, Braden."

There were little crinkles around his eyes when he smiled, but otherwise, he looked like the star I'd expected. Life on the road, touring all over the world, might have been a lucrative gig—but I could see it could take its toll, too.

"Feel free to call me Brade. All my friends do," he offered.

"Will do."

I followed him up some stairs. "We're heading to the game room. There will be some nice adult beverages for us there," he said over his shoulder.

And what a game room it was. There was a pool table, of course, and a sizeable poker table. There were also several leather sofas facing what looked to be a large movie screen. In the opposite corner was a nice wet bar, complete with a wall of shelves behind it holding every imaginable liquor and several I'd probably never even heard of. I settled into a stool at the bar while Brade walked behind it.

"What can I get you, my friend?" he asked, leaning on the bar.

"You got beer? I could go for a nice cold one."

"Coming right up." He popped the cap off a couple Stella Artois. We clinked bottles and each took a big swig.

"Great place you got here," I said.

Brade looked around, nodding. "Thank you. I like it, too. It's my sanctuary."

"Do your fans bother you here? Do they know you live here?" I asked.

"So far, it's been pretty quiet. I do have security, though. Cameras out front and shit."

"Wow. That's intense."

He nodded. "Yeah, it's kind of a drag, but there are crazies out there. You gotta be careful."

"So, what's our gathering all about tonight, do you know?" I asked when I noticed Maizy wasn't there yet

"Maizy told me she's been getting to know a few different guys, you and me included. She seemed not to know how to choose one out of the bunch, so I encouraged her to bring us all together."

"Okay. That's a unique approach."

"It is," he said, shrugging. "I thought it'd be cool to meet her other guys. I like her. I want her to be happy."

"Cheers to that," I said as we got started on our second round of beers.

The doorbell rang.

"That would be Maizy. Be right back." He disappeared down the stairs, leaving me to imagine what she might be wearing when she entered the room, and what she might be wearing underneath it.

As they mounted the stairs, I could hear her laugh getting nearer. Christ, the effect that woman had on me. My dick was already starting to come alive.

"Anson!" she said, running toward me with open arms. She was stunning as usual, with a sexy dress tied at the waist, which swung around her legs when she walked. She planted a big one on my lips, and when she hugged me, I took a deep inhale of her hair. God, she smelled great—classic, maybe Chanel?—mixed with something clean and fresh.

There was clearly no ice to break, there.

Brade went behind the bar and popped open champagne for Maizy and a couple more beers for us.

"Maizy, Anson tells me you work for his sister-in-law," Brade said.

Maizy rolled her eyes. "Yup."

"Yeah, Maiz, how's the old evil Eva? Still tormenting you at every turn?" I asked.

"God. You know it. Today she told me she didn't like my shoes."

Brade's mouth dropped open. "Get out of here. Your boss can say things like that to you?"

"Well, I don't know if she *can*. But she sure does. She's a piece of work. I can't imagine what she's like at family gatherings." She pushed her glasses up on her head and looked over at me.

"You do not want to know. Let's just leave it at that," I said, thinking back to a few choice holiday dinners that were memorable, and not in a good way.

"So, Maizy, why don't you tell us why you called us together?" Brade asked.

She cleared her throat. If I didn't know better, I would have sworn she was nervous.

Actually, I was nervous, myself. I had no idea what the hell to expect.

"Well, I've never been in this situation before, but I am dating some wonderful men." She paused to look both of us in the eyes. "I feel very lucky. But I am having a hard time knowing which one I really belong with—and which one wants to be with me. So I thought, if everyone were open to it, I'd bring us all together, and we could get to know each other that way."

"Cheers to that," Brade said. "Sounds kinda kinky, and I like kinky."

They looked to me. "It's unusual," I said slowly. "But I've actually done something like this before."

"Like what?" Brade asked.

"Dated a woman who my best friend was also dating."

Maizy looked surprised but Brade was unfazed. I guess when you're a rock star, you've seen everything.

"Yeah," I continued. "We both dated her until she decided she was more into him. They're still together. They're happy."

"That must have been rough, that she left you," Maizy said.

"I knew it could happen, going into it. I was happy for them."

"That's what I call love, brother," Brade said, extending his hand for what I call *the guy handshake*. "That you could look at their happiness and get happiness from it. That's what life's all about."

I hadn't really thought of it that way, but I guess he was right. And it had been a while since I'd *shared* a woman.

"That…is very interesting," Maizy said. I could tell the wheels were turning.

And I had a woman in front of me right then who I was dying to share.

"C'mere, baby," I said to Maizy. "Let me massage some of that worry out of your shoulders."

"Oh, yeah," she said, wedging herself between my knees where I sat on the barstool. With her back to me, she tapped her shoulders. "Right here, okay?"

"I gotcha." I looked over at Brade and gestured him over with a nod of my head.

He positioned himself right in front of her, and while I kneaded her tight shoulders, his hands wandered up to her great tits. He leaned in to kiss her. A moan passed from her lips as she gripped my thigh for balance. Her other hand reached for Brade.

As I worked her shoulders, I leaned forward into that gorgeous blonde hair of hers, just rubbing my face in it. My cock was rock-hard, and I scooted forward a bit on the barstool to press it into her ass. Seemed like she knew what I was up to, because she pushed her pretty little bum right back into me.

Brade looked at her. "Maizy, what do you say we all retire to the bedroom?"

She took a quick look back at me. "You good with that, Anson?"

"Oh, hell, yeah. Lead the way."

19

MAIZY

HOLY SHIT! I WAS ABOUT TO SLEEP WITH TWO GUYS.

Ohmygod.

To think all this started with my bitch boss telling me I'd be more respectable with a man by my side. Well, I wished she could have seen me then, about to get it on with not one, but two hotties.

Take that, Evil Eva.

I held hands with both guys as Brade steered us up another set of stairs to a killer bedroom. First off, the bed itself was gigantic—how convenient!—and encircled with a giant canopy thing of floaty fabric. The floor was covered in thick oriental rugs, and there were heavy dressers and a dreamy little reading nook over in the corner by the window.

I tried not to think about all the groupies who'd probably been in there before me. That was then.

This is now.

Before I could finish looking around, my slinky wrap dress was pulled over my head and thrown to the floor, leaving me standing in my nude thong and bra, thigh-high stockings, and four-inch high heels. In an instant, two pair of hands were wandering all over me, searing my skin with their heat, and leaving me with my head and heart in a twisted, confused, chaotic jumble of delight.

I moaned loudly when one of the guys—I think it was Brade—pushed my thong to the side and ran his fingers along the slit of my dripping pussy. I was so soaked for him—actually both of them—that I couldn't even see straight. I fumbled with someone's shirt buttons, my fingers clumsy as hell. I pushed the sleeves off two broad shoulders and bent to kiss and lick the strong chest right in front of me. Some sort of animal had taken over inside me. I was loving every minute of it.

While I was flicking nipples with my tongue, my hands wandered south to open a belt and fly, only to find someone going commando. A stiff dick popped into my hands while whoever was behind me continued to stroke me, back and forth, from clit to ass.

Speaking of which. I was pretty sure it was Anson behind me, and I was pretty sure he was playing with my ass. Holy cripes, I'd never gone there, or should I say, no guy'd ever gone there. But as weird as it felt, it was also freaking awesome, and I didn't want him to stop. Ever.

I kept my eyes closed, and all the sensation around me intensified. I didn't know what to do with two guys. What if they thought I was boring? Or unsexy? Or lame? Or fat?

Actually, I didn't care if they thought I was fat.

But so far, so good.

I rotated a half circle in my high heels so I had a fresh victim to undress. A new pair of lips fell on my mouth, so entirely different feeling and tasting, but just as thrilling as the one a moment before.

Shit. How did I get this freaking lucky?

This time, I went straight for the pants. In three seconds, I was sliding them down some rock-hard thighs, leaving me with another stiff cock bouncing off my burning skin.

Two hands came from behind to grasp my breasts, and those in front of me pulled me closer by grabbing the cheeks of my ass. I was sandwiched nice and tight between two hot as hell men. While the mouth of one bruised my lips, those of the other ravaged my neck. I figured I'd be covered with marks the next day, but that's what cover-up was for, right?

This new and unfamiliar bad girl naughtiness buzzed around my head like a noisy insect while four hands pillaged my sensitive body. I forced my eyes open and found myself facing my red-headed Anson.

"Hey there. You still with us?" he asked in a buttery voice.

"Mmmm," I said with half-lidded eyes.

"C'mon. Let's get you to the bed."

They lay me back. My legs were spread wide, and hands ran up and down the silky stockings I wore. My thong was pulled off, and a hot tongue commenced to plunder my tender pussy, my clit growing hard and erect. Anson sucked until I screamed.

I was powerless at the hands of these men. Holy lord.

Brade straddled my chest, his weight on his knees so he didn't squash me, and pushed my tits together. His hard dick slid between them and ground into me, gliding in and out. He gripped my girls so hard, it actually hurt, and adding insult to injury, he squeezed and rolled my nipples between his thumb and forefinger until I banged my head back against the bed. I dug my nails into his thighs. That only made him squeeze my tits harder.

I had to admit—I loved it.

He increased his speed, fucking my breasts like he was desperate. His breath came fast and hard.

"Fuck, Maizy, I'm gonna come on your tits," Brade groaned.

"Give it to me. Come on me," I begged.

With that, a searing, hot liquid surged between my breasts and up to my neck and chin. He continued pistoning while his cum dripped onto the bed below us. I managed to get some in my mouth and savored the tang I was now coated with.

"I want more," I moaned.

He moved off my chest and positioned his dick over my lips. I opened wide, and he lowered himself into my mouth so I could suck him clean. In the meantime, Anson worked his magic on my pussy. One finger entered me, rolling around in my juices. When fully seated inside me, he introduced another. His tongue continued to flick my clit, leaving me bucking my hips against his attentions.

Brade moved away from my mouth and positioned himself behind my head. He pulled my arms over my head, pinning them, and watching Anson work me over.

Fuck, it was all so hot.

Lightning shot through my every nerve as my orgasm built to a shattering explosion. My head lolled while my guys watched me come. I shuddered from head to toe, whimpering like a fool.

If I'd had any reservations about how these two would get along, they were gone now. The three of us could make quite the happy little family.

It was a shame I'd have to choose one to get my promotion. But life was a weird fucking game.

THE GUYS HAD CONKED out on the bed (two guys! in a bed! with me!), when I slipped out of the room and downstairs to call Sparkle.

"What?" she groaned.

Yeah, she'd been sleeping.

Whatever.

"Spark, I just slept with two guys," I whispered.

Why was I whispering? The guys were at the other end of the house, and besides, were dead to the world.

"WHAT?"

I had her attention now. All grogginess had left her voice.

"Maizy! I knew you had an inner slut. Was it good?"

"Ohmygod," was all I could say.

She yawned. "Well, I'm proud of you, big sis. It's something every woman should do at least once. Or, in my case, as often as possible." She giggled quietly.

"Is someone there?" I asked.

"Oh, yeah. Penn's here. He's asleep though. Oh, wait, I think he's waking up."

She gasped. "Oh…oh…"

Gross. I did not need to hear my sister get it on with Penn, the brother of the guy I'd just messed around with. As it was, I'd heard her screaming through the thin walls of our apartment on more than one occasion.

"Spark, I'm going now. Bye."

I hung up before she could respond with another moan.

I pulled the blanket I'd grabbed off the bed around me and nestled into the overstuffed sofa in Brade's living room. I was exhausted and a bit desperate for some sleep, but my mind was whirring at full speed.

I'd had plenty of sex before, probably even more than the average girl. I was good with that. But I'd not taken the *ménage* plunge, and there were still two more guys, Cato and Von, to add to the mix. Who would have thought that I, a serious, hard-working paralegal, would be in a twosome, a threesome, and maybe even a foursome?

Ha. If those judgmental fucks from the firm could see me now. I'd give them something to be scared of. They wanted me to pair off with a man in order to get my promotion?

Well, I'd pair off, all right. Just watch me.

20

BRADEN

WELL, DAMN.

I woke up in bed with my new buddy, Anson.

I wasn't too freaked to be waking up with a guy. After all, I was a rocker, and I'd been around. I'd had way more than my share of threesomes and more-somes, and if my sword crossed another dude's, I wasn't going to sweat it.

He seemed like an alright guy. And he sure did work over Maizy.

Speaking of which, where the hell was she? I slipped out of bed, grabbed a thick bathrobe that had been a gift from someone—my manager or the record label, I couldn't remember which—and slipped out of my bedroom.

And there she was, in the downstairs living room,

looking like a small and innocent angel, curled up on my massive sofa with a huge blanket wrapped tightly around her. Her blonde hair was splayed everywhere like a massive, crazy wave. I wanted to bury my face in it, but first, I watched her sleep. She shifted, pulling the blanket tighter, and made the slightest snoring sound. God, she was sweet.

And I was whipped.

There was no way she could know that, of course. At least, I hoped she didn't know. Not yet, anyway. *But I knew.*

There'd been something there the first time we met, when I thought she was a secretary at the law firm. Yeah, that had been a dick move on my part, to open my big mouth like I had. But the way she handled it, like someone who was a pro at dealing with assholes, just slayed me. As much of a douche as I acted like, she didn't lose her shit. She kept her eye on the prize—keeping her client calm and happy—and I had huge respect for that.

When my band was nothing more than a piss-ant operation playing dive bars and county fairs, it was easy to get down. I was tempted to throw in the towel many a time. The guys and I had any number of petty disagreements—disagreements that would tear a weaker band apart. But we didn't let that happen to us. Just like Maizy, we *kept our eyes on the prize.*

I knew how hard it could be to do that. And I knew how it could also pay off.

And since that time, there had been untold masses of women who'd come and gone. It was weird as hell, and I wasn't sure I'd ever understand it, but chicks *threw* themselves at entertainers. Athletes, too. It was the stupidest thing. I mean, the vast majority of us are some of the biggest assholes on the planet. What was in it for the ladies? I just didn't get it.

But I was the happy beneficiary of their strange fetish. And I took full advantage of it. I fucked more babes than Hugh Hefner, and somehow, miraculously, walked away with no diseases and no pregnancies.

I was tired of it, though. Tired of the groupies, tired of the anonymous sex, tired of touring. It was time for a break. And time for some changes.

Time to get to know this hot paralegal who used to be in a girl band.

I pictured how she'd writhed on the bed when Anson went to town on her. God, I didn't think I'd ever seen anything like it, such a beautiful woman letting herself go, enjoying having her pussy licked. And damn if my dick didn't start to come to life just then, watching her snooze.

She flipped over on the sofa with a small moan, and the blanket traveled with her, leaving her pretty little ass exposed. Christ, that gave me a full-on woody. I reached inside my robe and stroked myself slowly, squeezing the head of my cock just the way I liked it.

I walked over to the sofa and got on my knees to get closer to Maizy. I took a deep inhale, and everything about her smelled like heaven. Even the slight scent of sex on her made my hard-on rage. I lowered the blanket slightly to brush my lips across her bare shoulder and watched her skin light up with goose bumps. She stirred and, still sleeping, flipped back over on the sofa, facing me. I bent to kiss her lips, and her eyes slowly fluttered open.

"Hey, gorgeous," I whispered.

She looked around for a second, and when she realized where she was, looked back at me with a sleepy smile. "Hey, yourself," she said.

"Looks like you might be naked under that blanket there."

She lifted it and took a quick peek. "I might be. What about it?"

"Well, I was thinking of dropping this robe and crawling under there with you. Ya know, just for some snuggling."

"I'd be down with that." She flipped back the blanket to make room for me, in the process giving me a perfect view of her perfect tits and shaved pussy. Man, I liked shit like that.

I squeezed onto the sofa with her. There wasn't a ton of room, so we had to lie pressed together. No problem there. My dick, of course, was standing at full attention, and when I pressed it into her stomach, she gasped, sending a spark through my veins. What was it about this girl?

I reached down to finger her, moving slowly to

make sure she was ready after our last session. When she pressed her hips into my hand, she answered my question.

She was not only ready. She was hungry. For me.

My cock was throbbing, and as if she knew, she reached to stroke my length, the very same cock that just a few hours earlier had come all over her lovely tits.

I parted her pussy lips and ran my fingers along her soft folds, sticky from our earlier play. She moaned, melting into my touch, and her lips swelled with arousal.

"You good, baby?" I asked, her breath deepening from my strokes.

"Yeah," she whispered. "Could you fuck me, Brade? Please?"

She didn't need to ask twice.

I popped up off the sofa and opened a lacquered box on my coffee table. From it, I grabbed a condom, rolling the bad boy over my stiff one. I returned to the sofa, lying alongside Maizy, where I lifted her top leg into the crook of my arm. With my lips on her mouth, I eased the head of my cock into her entrance, giving her time to adjust. As soon as she relaxed and opened up for me, I could no longer hold back. Fortunately, I didn't need to.

"Fuck, baby. Can I give it all to you now?" I asked.

"Please. Please fuck my pussy," she begged, her chest rising and falling as her control slipped away.

She tilted her hips to give me more access, and I raised her leg up higher, giving her every last inch of my cock until I was balls-deep inside. I ground my teeth to keep from exploding, and damn if I didn't feel like I'd died and gone to heaven. Her juicy pussy gripped me like a tight glove, and I plunged in and out as deeply as I could.

"Oh, oh, oh…" she screamed as she contracted around my cock.

"You coming, baby? You coming on my cock?"

"Y…yeh…yes…," was all she could manage.

I drove into her faster and faster until an orgasm shattered what was left of her composure. My own willpower gave way, and I exploded, cum shooting from my balls. Even though I was wearing a condom, I swear I could feel every bit of the grip of her delicious pussy.

It was all new territory for me, sex that was more than the purely physical and passing. Yeah, I wanted to fuck Maizy's brains out, but I also wanted to learn everything about her—who her friends were, what she liked and didn't like, what made her laugh and what made her cry. I wanted her on my arm, but I knew the choice was hers to make, and that it wasn't going to be an easy one for her. I'd be lying if I didn't say I hoped she'd choose me, but in the end, what mattered most was that she was as happy as humanly possible. Everything else was gravy.

"Wow," she murmured. "What just happened?"

I kissed her again, unable to separate from the sweetness of her lips. That was what a kiss was supposed to be like. And it hadn't been that way for me in a long, long time.

I planted one more on her honeyed little lips. "This is what I call just getting started."

21

MAIZY

So now I knew what all the fuss was about. Sex with two guys was freaking amazing. All I could think about was when I might be able to do it again.

But since I was at work, I pushed that out of my mind. I had a meeting with none other than Brade and my boss, Eva. I'd just about wrapped everything up, but Eva wanted to formalize things. We giggled about it beforehand, Brade and I, joking that we'd like to tie Eva up and watch us get it on.

I hoped she wouldn't embarrass me in front of him, but on the other hand, I hoped she'd try to do just that. I was fully confident that Brade would put her in her place with a perfect smack-down she wouldn't be able to respond to. She'd have to eat it, because *he* was the client. If she chased him off with her bitchiness, we could lose his business. That would not be good for the firm, because Brade paid them a nice monthly retainer to take care of his legal crap, and it would be disastrous for her. She could lose her job.

Which might not be such a bad thing…

So it was no surprise that when I ushered him into her office to go over his case, she turned into an insufferable bootlicker. She always did this with clients, but it seemed amplified with Brade, I guess because he was a rock star. Apparently, she was a huge fan, which was probably why she'd refreshed her lipstick and finger-combed her severe bob.

"Braden, I just wanted to have a quick meeting and see how we're progressing with your case. I know Maizy's been taking good care of you," she said.

If she only knew *how* I'd been taking care of him…

Brade looked over at me, giving away nothing. He was so hot in his faded jeans and leather jacket. But being the professional I was, I just pushed my glasses up on my nose and nodded politely.

"Yeah, Maizy's taking care of everything," he said.

She should have been asking me, but whatever. I just smiled.

Eva looked at me like she doubted I was capable of tying my shoe. God, she was a bitch. She *knew* I was doing a *great* job but just had to make it clear she was the head honcho.

She nodded at Brade. "Okay, then. Glad to hear all

is well. Maizy is quite capable, but if you ever need anything, you know how to reach me."

Braden stood. He had no patience for boring pleasantries.

"Thank you, Eva." He extended his hand.

Her mouth opened but quickly closed. She was normally the one to call a meeting to a close.

"I see you have a show coming up here in the city, next week," she said, placing her folded hands under her chin.

Was she also batting her eyes?

Ugh. She was hinting for free tickets. Could she have been any more obvious?

Brade nodded, glancing at me. "Yes, I do. I think tickets are still available. I hope you can make it."

Boo-yah. He'd given me *free* tickets! Not that I'd share that with Eva.

"Well, we'll see you there," she said with a forced smile on her face.

"Thanks, Eva," I said, moving toward the door. I couldn't get him out of there fast enough.

I walked him to the elevator before I went back to my cube.

Brade lowered his voice. "Yeah, she was a little bitchy. It was like the air smelled of it."

I had to laugh at that.

He took a discreet hold of my fingers and squeezed.

"See you later, then?" he asked.

"Looking forward to it," I said, sad to say even a temporary goodbye to my sexy rocker boy.

WRAPPING myself in my trench coat, I slipped past Eva's office. Well, I tried to, anyway. There was no way to avoid her when it was quitting time, and I knew the chances of her stopping me with some stupid question or nasty insult were about fifty-fifty. But I needed to get the hell out of there and home. I had Cato and Von coming over for dinner to meet each other. I was a bundle of nerves and wanted to make sure I got the cooking mostly done before they arrived and I got all distracted.

"Maizy!" she called out in a cheerful voice.

Busted.

I stopped at her door, displaying my most pleasant smile. "Eva," I said, like I was super glad to see her. God, I should win an acting award. "How was your day?" Like I cared.

Ignoring my question, she said, "C'mon in, Maizy. Have a seat." She gestured toward the chair I always sat in, as if I didn't know I could sit there. The fact that I was holding my bag and had my coat on went completely unnoticed.

I took a super-quick glance at my watch, not long enough to say "I have somewhere better to be" because you can't do that with your boss, but rather a glance that said something along the lines of "Where did the day go?"

But it made no difference. She couldn't give a crap about any schedule I might have to keep.

"Good meeting with Braden today, don't you think?" she asked.

I nodded. Of course it was a good meeting. What the hell else did she expect?

"Yes, I'd say very good. We're getting his royalties taken care of without any protracted legal action. I think he's very happy with the firm's work." I'd already told her these things, multiple times, so I wasn't sure what else to say.

What was she getting at?

She walked around her desk toward me and propped her ass on its corner, trying to be all casual and stuff.

"You know, Maizy, I sensed something in today's meeting."

Oh, shit.

Stay cool.

"What do you mean, Eva?" I opened my eyes so wide it nearly hurt. I was going for the innocent look.

She furrowed her brow. "Well, I'm not entirely sure, but I think Braden might have taken a liking to you."

No shit, Sherlock.

But I protested with a laugh and wave of my hand.

"Oh, don't I wish, Eva. Imagine, a rock star interested in me."

Indeed.

She tilted her head. "Yes. You're probably right. I can't imagine why he would be interested in someone like you."

There was the sting I'd been waiting for. She never freaking failed. But I kept my cool and didn't let my "pleasant smile" falter.

"So what's up with my brother-in-law?" she asked.

Shit. I should have known she'd go there.

"Oh, um, I think we may get together again, soon," I said.

Should I have told her how he went down on me the night before, played with my ass, came in my mouth?

Nah.

She nodded, like she was thinking. "Glad to hear it. This could be very good for your position here at the firm, you know, if anything comes of it."

"Well, fingers crossed," I said, holding up my crossed fingers. I stood. "Was there anything else, Eva?"

She looked distracted. For Christ's sake, I wished she spit out whatever was on her mind.

"I was surprised Braden didn't offer us any free tickets to his show."

There it was.

As if she couldn't afford to buy her own. What a

cheapskate. And no, I wasn't about to let her know I got freebies. Backstage passes, too, bitch.

I inched toward the door. "I guess they only get so many free tickets."

She crossed her arms, her face screwed up with thought. Christ, was it that big of a deal to her? She needed to get a life.

"I suppose." Spell broken, she walked back behind her desk. "See you tomorrow," she said, dismissing me without looking up.

FINALLY HOME, I smiled as I passed the painting Anson had bought me at his friend's gallery. It was the perfect piece for my foyer and best of all, I saw it every day when I went in and out of my apartment. And thought of him, too, of course.

Throwing my things aside, I tied on an apron to protect my work clothes. The pizza dough I'd made the night before came out of the fridge, along with several different toppings, and the oven was set to five hundred degrees. The cork on the Chianti Classico was pulled, and I set three wine glasses out. The gelato maker was switched to *on* and filled with the pistachio mixture I'd also made the night before. I had even warned Sparkle, that if she came around, to make sure she was fully dressed. I was ready.

And not a moment too soon. My bell rang, and there stood Cato at the door, looking even more handsome than he had the other night at his boss's penthouse.

What a night that had been.

"Hey, handsome," I said, letting him in. "I barely saw you all day."

He hooked his finger under my chin and tipped up my face for a delicious kiss.

"With this new job at the firm, it's amazing I ever see the light of day."

I took his hand and led him to the kitchen.

Handing him a glass of wine, I said, "I appreciate your being open about this. You know, meeting the others."

"Happy to support the cause," he said, settling into a barstool at my counter and raising his glass in a toast.

But something in his tone didn't ring true. I turned to the sink to wash the vegetables and hide my face at the same time. His words had brought tears to my eyes. The last thing in the world I wanted to do was hurt Cato. My dear, dear Cato.

Was I being selfish in bringing the guys together? I'd gone into it with the best of intentions.

Shit.

But it was too late now. The wheels were in motion. They all knew about each other, and they'd all soon meet. The best thing I could do was be honest.

So I walked over to Cato.

"Hey," I said, snuggling up to the stool where he sat.

"Hey, yourself," he said, pulling off his glasses and setting them on the countertop. He'd loosened his tie, and goddamn if he wasn't the epitome of the guy at work you most wanted to fuck.

I ran my hand along his thigh. "I don't want this to be a bad experience. I know it seems unorthodox. The last thing I want to do is hurt you."

He looked down at his wine.

I'd been right. There *was* something eating at him.

His gaze returned to mine. "I've had feelings for you for so long. I'd always hoped it would some day be the two of us."

He might as well just have stabbed me in the heart. Because it sure as hell felt like it.

22

CATO

I DIDN'T WANT TO MAKE MAIZY FEEL BAD. I REALLY didn't. But I'd set my sights on dating her so long ago, that now we were finally coming together, I wasn't thrilled about being one of four. She had to choose one, and if I were perfectly honest, I wanted it to be me. The other guys might be great, but I didn't really want to see her with them.

I wanted to see her with *me*.

You couldn't blame me, really.

But I wasn't going to be a dick about it. If she wanted us to get to know each other, hang out, even become friends, I was fine with that. On the positive side, it was going to be great to hang out with someone other than attorneys. I was the only scumbag lawyer in the group, thank god.

Anyway, I upset her with my big mouth when I told her I'd wanted her for myself. Now I felt like a shit.

"Hey, Maizy, c'mon. It's all good, everything will work out. Look—at the very least, we'll always be good friends," I said, ruffling her hair. "I mean, work would be unbearable without you."

She looked at me with a small but grateful smile. The Chianti was making me warm and relaxed, so I pulled her to me. Her lips parted just in time to greet my exploring tongue. God, she was delicious.

We were interrupted by the doorbell.

Of course.

When she pulled away from me to go answer it, I looked around the apartment. I'd never been there before. It was a typical small New York apartment, but it was nice in a girl-ish sort of way—overstuffed furniture and lots of scented candles and throw pillows.

Maizy came bounding into the kitchen, all smiles, holding the hand of a tall dude, who must have been Von, who had two dogs on leashes. He walked right up to me, hand extended.

"I'm Von, great to meet you. I understand you two work together. You must have a lot of fun."

"Hey, man. Nice to meet you. And I wish the place we worked was fun," I said, shaking my head.

He laughed.

"But we do our best to stick together and not let the bullshit get us down."

I got down on my knees to greet the dogs. They

were big, happy mutts, and when Von clicked his tongue, they both sat back on their haunches.

"You trained them well. Look at that," I said, returning to standing to watch the dogs fight their urge to jump all over me.

Von reached to pat them on their heads. "They're good boys. All the dogs are for the most part, but these guys are the best behaved. That's why I brought them tonight." They looked up at him, then at me, and then back at him.

"Chianti?" Maizy asked, handing a glass to Von.

"Oh, yeah, I need this. I had a hell of a day," he said.

"Hey, you're a vet, right?" I asked.

He nodded. "Yes, I am. Got my own practice across town. And today was a crazy one."

"He also is a sucker for taking in stray animals," Maizy said with a smile.

I raised my glass in toast to him. "Can't blame a guy for that."

He raised his glass back. "Better be careful. I can be very persuasive about getting people to adopt animals who need homes."

"So what happened at work?" Maizy asked.

Von settled onto the stool next to me.

"Someone discovered one of those nasty puppy mills and rescued the dogs. There were about ten of them, and half came to my practice and half went to my buddy's practice. Poor babies were a mess." He shook his head.

"God, I can't believe people do that to dogs. Fuckers," I said.

"It's unbelievable. We got them cleaned up with a flea bath, dressed the sores they had, gave them their shots, and fed them probably the first good meal they'd had since they were taken away from their mothers."

"Wow. That's incredible. I assume you probably don't get paid for work like that, do you?" I asked, feeling like a shit for spending my days doing legal work for rich assholes.

"Nope. You're right. It's pro bono. But I have a pretty busy practice so I can absorb it. It's just tiring when you squeeze in cases like this in addition to the day's appointments." He looked over at Maizy, who was putting what looked like homemade pizza in the oven. "It's time to perk up now, though. Work is behind me, and I am very happy to be here. And that food looks killer."

"Cheers to that," I said. We all clinked our glasses together.

Maybe this wasn't going to be such a bad deal. Von seemed cool, and I really respected his commitment to his work. You had to hand it to someone who loved animals that much.

Maizy walked over and stood before the two of us, looking cute as hell in her little apron. I'd never considered aprons hot before, but my dick let me know this girl had gotten my attention.

"Okay. The pizza will be out in about three minutes.

Then I'll pop another one in, and we'll eat," she said, placing a hand on each of our thighs.

Fuck the pizza. I saw something before me that I was much hungrier for. I pulled her toward me for a kiss, and then directed her to Von.

I wasn't going to be the asshole who bogarted the girl. As much as I might have liked to.

But to be honest, my dick did a double twitch when I watched her kiss Von. I certainly didn't expect *that* to be a turn-on. But shit, it was hot.

Interesting.

When she finished kissing him, she gave me a look that just about killed. It was sweet but also seductive as hell. Like she knew that my watching her kiss him would get me going.

How had she known that?

She was making her way back over to me when the kitchen timer went off.

Oh, well. There'd be plenty of time for fun later.

I stole a look at Von, who just looked happy as hell and completely unbothered by the fact that there was another dude there who'd also just kissed his girl.

I guess you just never know.

He saw me looking at him.

"So what about you, Cato? What's up with your work at the firm? Maizy's told me what a high stress place it can be."

I took a deep breath and nodded. "Yeah. They're working me hard. I mean, this is the first socializing

I've done in probably two or three weeks. I don't usually get out of the office 'til nine or so."

What a douche I was. Here was this guy who'd totally followed his passion. At the end of a day, he was exhausted, but he could go to bed knowing he'd done the world some good.

Not so much the case for me.

"That sounds rough, dude," Von said.

"Yeah. I'm trying to figure out if it's for me. I'm pretty sure it's not. I just have to think about next steps, like what else I'd rather do. That sort of thing."

"I'm sure you'll get it figured out. Our girl here, though, she likes the work she does at the firm. Isn't that right, baby?" he asked.

She finished putting the food on the table and waived us over. "I do like the work I do. It's not nearly as grueling as Cato's. But my boss is a piece of work."

Jesus, did her pizzas look incredible. I almost ran to the table. I couldn't remember if I'd eaten all day.

Maizy was an amazing cook, as I'd somehow known she would be. She was good at almost everything she did. It was one of the things I loved about her.

Shit. Love?

She'd added to my life in so many ways, not least of which was helping me come out of my shell at work. I mean, sure, I was recognized for the results I produced, but I was just shy enough to want to avoid anything to do with small talk or socializing with others there. She'd shown me how to relax and trust myself in those situations. Whenever the familiar twinge of discomfort crept up on me, I just pictured her face.

Her beautiful face. Which I happened to be looking at right now.

The assholes at the firm looked down on her, which really chapped my ass. None of them had an ounce of the character she did. Just because she hadn't gone to a fancy university and was a paralegal instead of an attorney, they thought they were better.

But they weren't.

Of that, I was sure.

23

MAIZY

HOLY LORD, I HAD TWO GORGEOUS MEN IN MY apartment, and they were devouring my cooking. What girl wouldn't love that? I just hoped Sparkle stayed out for a while longer so I could really show these two a good time.

The best part was that they seemed to enjoy each other's company. No tension. No animosity. At least, none that was visible to me.

"Damn, this pizza is amazing," Von said. "I've never had homemade pizza."

His pups watched from the corner of the living room. They were perfectly obedient but clearly tormented by the smells filling the apartment. I felt better when he threw them a few treats from his pocket.

"Where'd you learn to make pizza like this?" Cato asked.

I had to admit, I was pretty proud of my pizza-making abilities.

"I took a class, and then practiced a lot. It was a little tricky to get the super-thin crust but after I made it about a dozen times, I had it down." What I didn't say was that while I was perfecting my pizza, Sparkle and I happily ate the ones that were less than perfect. They were still absolutely delicious.

Something inside me enjoyed that I'd impressed the guys with my cooking. I wanted them to see that I had a lot of dimensions, and that I was more than just a girl who worked at a law firm. Who was sleeping with four guys.

Cato cleared the table when we'd finished, and I brought out fruit and my fresh-made gelato.

"Shall we move over to the living room?" I suggested.

"Let's do it," Von said, as Cato nodded in agreement.

We settled in, and I looked at both guys, first one, and then the other as we shoveled the frozen goodness into our mouths.

"Thank you for coming tonight," I said. "I know this might seem odd, but I wanted the men who were really important to me, to meet."

"How'd it go last night?" Von asked.

I blushed. Shit.

They looked at each other and laughed.

"Okay, okay. Anson, Brade, and I had fun. My next step, after tonight, is to get all five of us together and see how that goes."

"Sounds good to me," Von said, raising his glass in a toast.

Cato, on the other hand, was silent for a moment. He was thoughtful, and if I knew anything about him, it was that he never spoke until he was sure of what he wanted to say.

"I agree," he said, leaving me a little shocked. "It's all good."

Whoa. Was he just saying that to placate me, or did he mean it?

We'd find out in just a few minutes.

"In fact," he continued, "I've got an idea." He looked from me, to Von, and back.

"What?" I asked. "What do you have up your sleeve?"

"Why don't you go take all your clothes off and come back wearing just the apron? And your heels, of course."

Oh, my. He was a little dirty bird.

I stood. "I think that's a lovely idea. You guys chat, and I'll be back in a few minutes."

I CLOSED the door to my bedroom, and before undressing as Cato had demanded, I dialed Sparkle.

"Hey, girl," she answered on the last ring.

"Hey. Guess what. I think I'm about to have another threesome. Two nights in a row," I said.

"Dayum, sissy. You're a big old whore, aren't you?"

"Hey. I learned from the best."

"Ha. You're funny. Which guys are there tonight?" she asked.

"Cato and Von."

"Nice. Very nice," she said.

"So, we're gonna be…you know…"

"Yeah. I know. I'll stay out. Just keep off my bed."

"That's gross. I would never mess around on your bed."

"Okay, ho bag. Talk to you later. Have fun."

"Hey, before you go," I said.

"Yeah?"

"Well. I feel kind of bad." Damn, there was that old familiar lump in my throat. "I actually like them all. A lot. I'm scared."

Sparkle's deep sigh came through loud and clear over the phone. She might have a weird, hippy-dippy perspective on the world, but she was never one to mince words and was always honest to a fault. She would *always* tell you when your butt looked big.

"Are you telling them about the promotion thing?" she asked.

"I don't know. I mean, I have to at some point. Cato knows. He's the only one."

"You know my motto," she said simply.

It was true. I did know her "motto."

"Yeah. Honesty."

"Yeah, sissy. You need to be honest. Bring them all together and talk to them."

Was she crazy?

Maybe, but I also knew she was right. I might end up with no guy and no promotion, but I suppose I wouldn't be any worse off than I was when I'd started. Which really wasn't such a horrible starting place, if you thought about it.

I TOOK MY TIME UNDRESSING, pressing my ear to the bedroom door to hear how the guys were getting on in the living room.

Geez. It was like they were long-lost friends. They were swapping stories of their travels to Machu Picchu. I wasn't even sure they missed me.

So I took the time to brush out my hair, gargle, and touch up my makeup. I removed all my clothes except my lacy boy-cut panties and put the apron back on over them. Checking myself out in the mirror, I had to say, I looked pretty damn good. The sides of my boobs were peeking out from the apron, and the bottom hem barely covered my crotch. I popped my heels back on, took a deep breath, and returned to the living room.

"Damn," Von hissed when he saw me.

"Dude," Cato said.

I approached them as slowly as I could, although I really would have loved to run and throw myself at them—Cato in his shirt sleeves and loosened tie, and Von in his outdoorsy, casual duds. Both buff, and hot as hell.

"Hey," I said in a soft voice.

They both leaned back on the sofa, hands behind their heads. They studied me with a heated intensity that made me shake, as if I were prey they were stalking. Craving pulsed through me as they looked me up and down like hungry animals.

Or was it the other way around?

I wanted to please them with every fiber of my being.

Von twirled his finger. "Turn around for us, baby."

I rotated in my high heels, one tiny step at a time to draw out the suspense. Their heavy gazes seared my flesh, leaving me starving for touch. It was time to ratchet up the fun.

With a little strip tease.

I was facing away, with my back to them. I glanced over my shoulder and hooked my thumbs in my panties, which I lowered just an inch, swaying enough to mesmerize the guys with my ass.

One sucked in his breath. The other released a small *mmmm.*

I lowered the lacy fabric more, leaning forward just enough to stick my behind in their direction, and pushed the rest of my panty below my ass cheeks. I squirmed to make sure they were getting a good, long look.

I glanced back again and saw Von adjusting himself. The magic was working.

Not that I ever had any doubts.

When my panties reached the floor, I bent deeply to throw them aside. While folded forward, I stepped my feet a few inches apart to give them a perfect view of my most private parts.

"Fuck, baby," Cato groaned.

Could they see how soaked I was? I hoped so.

Emboldened by something I couldn't identify, I reached between my legs and ran a finger between my pussy lips, dragging my moisture from one end of my slit to another. I slowly straightened back up, the blood having rushed to my head, and turned back around to face them.

But not before I scooped my panties up off the floor and threw them to Von.

He smiled and brought them to his face. His gaze locked with mine, and he took a deep inhale of the lacy fabric. He tossed it aside and extended his hand to me.

I approached the sofa, taking Von's hand and stroking Cato's beautiful face.

"Are you ready for us, darlin'?" Von asked.

A tremor of anticipation swam through me. "Are you ready for *me*?"

The guys looked at each other with big smiles. This was my show, and we all knew it.

I knelt before Cato, clamoring for what I knew would be a very hard cock buried in a tangle of boxers and trousers. When I had freed his erection, I pulled it toward my mouth, savoring the drop of precum on his tip. I ran my lips all the way down to the root.

Von got up from the sofa and positioned himself behind my bare ass, now that I was bent over in service to Cato.

Von's fingers smoothed over my sensitive core, using barely enough pressure to part my lips. One finger dipped between them, spreading my slickness from side to side. I shimmied with pleasure, sucking Cato harder.

"Shit, baby," Cato murmured, his head lolling back onto the sofa. He tangled his fingers in my hair and pushed me deeper onto his cock, his demanding touch leaving my head spinning. All I could think of was pleasing him, and I sucked him until he banged the back of my throat.

And, there was Von, who so expertly tormented me with his decadent attentions. I pushed my hips back toward him to give more of myself, and he growled his appreciation. His thumbs opened me and next thing I knew, his tongue was buried deep inside me. If my mouth hadn't been full of Cato's cock, I would have screamed loudly enough for the neighbors and the people in the building next door to hear, too.

Cato's breath grew raspy, and his grip tightened in my hair.

"Goddamn, baby. I'm so fucking hard for you." He lifted his head from the sofa. "Yes…yeah…suck me…"

He growled, which gave way to a heady moan, and I tasted the first explosion of his hot cum. I swallowed as it blasted through my mouth, allowing only a drop or two to escape my lips and run down my chin. I continued pistoning him as he threw his head back and forth and hollered a litany of profanities. I licked him clean as he came down.

And while he did, my own orgasm at Von's touch built to an earth-shattering crescendo. I shoved my hips back into his mouth, and he, in turn, lapped at me with a vigor that left me coming all over his gorgeous face.

Cato pulled me up on the sofa, cradling me in his arms. How did I end up with these two men who treated me like a queen? A flash of discomfort washed over me as I remembered having been with Brade and Anson the night before.

But there'd be time to worry about that later. I wanted to give these amazing men all the attention they deserved, and then some.

"Looks like we wore the girl out," Von said.

I forced my eyes opened and gave each of them a look.

"That'll never happen," I said in a dreamy voice.

Cato smoothed some sweaty strands of hair off my face. "We'll just see about that," he added.

24

VON

Maizy's heated passion blew my mind, not to mention what it did to my dick. Shit, I was ready to get down on one knee and make an honest woman of her.

Except that I was one of four. Four guys, who I was pretty sure were all vying for her commitment.

I didn't have a problem with that, per se. I wasn't a possessive or jealous guy. Lord knew I was busy as hell with my veterinary practice, so would probably be a shitty boyfriend, anyway. But I wouldn't have minded giving it a shot.

If she chose me.

Which she might not.

But hell, as long as she was happy, I'd be happy. And as long as Cher the rat was alive, I'd probably have the chance to see the lovely Maizy from time to time.

I hustled to the kitchen to get us all water and returned to find Maizy slowly unfolding herself from Cato's lap, disheveled as hell with her hair in knots, her previously starched apron wrinkled and askew.

Just how I liked her.

"Mmmm," she said, stretching. "Let's go to bed."

Cato and I looked at each other, then looked to Maizy.

"Um. Both of us?" Cato asked.

She nodded sleepily. "Yeah. C'mon."

I raised my eyebrows at Cato, who shrugged in return.

If this was what our girl wanted, then what the hell. We could do this.

She reached for our hands, leading us to her bedroom like a pro, her eyes sparkling with contentment. We crawled under her down comforter, with her in the middle, of course, and held her hands while she dozed off. The dogs never made a peep. I'd have to thank them later for their excellent cooperation.

I waited for Maizy's breathing to grow slow and steady, and then I mouthed the words I'd been thinking all evening, which led me to wonder.

Did the other guys feel the same way about her?

THE NEXT DAY at work passed as planned—busy as hell, which I was glad about because it kept me from thinking about Maizy. I had just two more cats to examine, and then I could wrap things up, get home to shower, and dash uptown to Braden Darby's place where all five of us would be together for the first time. In spite of the strangeness of the situation, I was looking forward to it. Don't ask me why. Something about Maizy made it easier to emerge from the old comfort zone.

The orange tabby I was treating yawned in my face, and I yawned right back in his.

Maizy would be delighted to know how I exhausted I was. Not that I wouldn't repeat the last evening all over again—hell, I didn't think I would ever say no to that woman. I couldn't fathom how any man would. But it was a good thing I did most of my work standing up because if I'd sat down for five minutes, I would've passed out, sound asleep.

It turned out that when Maizy was with two guys—and maybe more, time would tell—she was nearly insatiable. I mean, there was no doubt she was one of the most passionate women I'd ever been with, but when she put Cato and me together, well, she could barely function aside from getting down to business. How she'd managed to get through dinner and clean up, I'd never know.

After a brief snooze of fifteen minutes on her part,

she was awake once again. Cato and I spend almost the entire night taking turns eating her pussy, fucking her, and having her suck us off until I personally couldn't take any more and went out to the sofa to get a couple hours' sleep. I wasn't too successful, however, as Cato kept her going until the sun came up, their noise probably keeping the entire building awake. Those two were going to have fun at work the next day, exhausted, but knowing each other's most intimate touch. I had to smile when I thought about it. And with a strange lack of jealousy, too. Go figure.

Myself, I would be enjoying smelly dogs all day. But that was okay. I liked smelly dogs.

When I'd finally gotten home through rush hour traffic, my place was dead silent—the pups must have been out with the dog walker. As much as I loved my four-legged friends, sometimes it was nice to come home to total silence. Of course, I was never *actually* alone thanks to the cats, but they didn't have the tendency to get in my face the way the pooches did.

Stepping out of the shower, I pulled on my boxers. Damn if my bed didn't look like the most tempting thing in the world at that moment, but I powered through and finished getting dressed. I was expected at Braden's and would never let Maizy down. I figured I'd be able to um, rise to the occasion if the opportunity presented itself. Which I hoped it would.

My Uber pulled up to drop me in front of Braden's

place, a gorgeous brownstone that must have cost millions. I loved where I lived, absolutely, but there was something so regal about the city's huge old townhouses, especially the ones that had not been carved up into rabbit-warren apartment buildings.

I was pretty sure Braden Darby's brownstone was intact and had not been at the mercy of greedy landlords.

The front door swung open, and I was greeted by none other than the rock star himself, a slim guy with shoulder length dirty blond hair.

"You must be Von. Call me Brade," he said, offering his hand and leading me into a massive foyer. "What can I get you to drink?"

"Thanks, man. What are you drinking?" I asked, following him into a massive kitchen already populated with one other guy who must have been Anson, and of course our girl Maizy.

"Scotch. Would you like a scotch?" he asked.

"That would be great." I should probably have been asking for coffee, but what the hell. I could sleep when I was dead.

I caught Maizy's eye as I entered the room and she ran to me, throwing her arms around my neck and planting a big one on my lips.

Man, I could get used to that.

I held her at arm's length so I could take her in. She was a stunner by any measure, but her warmth and sex appeal were something that had to be witnessed first-hand, revealing itself in the way she moved, smiled, and was just plain sweet.

"You look gorgeous, baby," I said.

And she did, with her mass of hair twisted into a messy braid that hung over her right shoulder, a slim, pinstriped skirt, and a sleeveless blouse that showed off her toned arms. But it was the glasses that got me.

On anyone else, they would have been just goofy and oversized. But on her, shit, they looked like a million bucks. She looked smart as hell. Which of course, she was. I couldn't take my eyes off her until she snapped me out of my reverie.

"Von, you haven't met Anson yet," she said, introducing me to a tall guy with red hair.

"Right," I said, coming back to my senses. "Sorry for being rude, Anson. I just couldn't take my eyes off our girl here."

He shook my hand with a big smile. "I'm with you on that, my man."

I looked around the kitchen.

"Hey, where's Cato? He's joining us, right?" I asked.

"Yeah, but he's running late," Maizy said. "His boss threw something at him when he was ready to head out the door."

Anson shook his head. "Guess that's why lawyers get paid the big bucks."

For all the sacrifices Cato seemed to make, I wasn't

sure any amount of big bucks would be worth it. But he'd figure it out. He was a smart guy.

"Awesome place you have here, Brade," I said, looking around. It made me want to re-think my own apartment. Not that I could afford a brownstone, but I loved the traditional touches like the picture rail and coffered ceiling. And the walls were covered in awesome modern and abstract art, which was the perfect contrast.

Brade looked around. "Thanks, Von. Yeah, this is my sanctuary. Sometimes I never want to leave."

"Do fans ever bother you here?" I asked. Probably a douche thing to ask, but if Maizy was going to hang out here, I wanted to know she'd be safe.

Brade nodded. "I've had the occasional fan show up at my door. But I've got pretty tight security. You probably didn't notice the cameras when you came in. And there's a security guy in the basement office at all times. Well, at least when I'm in town."

I shook my head. "I should have known you'd have it covered. Dumb question. Sorry, man."

"No, I'm glad you asked. You have a right to," Brade said.

Someone's cell phone clattered on the marble counter, and Maizy reached for hers.

"Oh, good news. Cato will be here shortly," she said with a huge smile.

Brade poured me another finger of scotch. "So, shall

we head up to the game room? It's my favorite place to hang."

"I can vouch for that," Anson said. "It's amazing and has great views."

We headed up the stairs and as soon as we settled in, the doorbell rang.

Brade excused himself.

Anson turned to Maizy. "So, how was your day? My evil sister-in-law give you any crap?"

"Wait," I said, looking between the two of them. "You work for Anson's sister-in-law?"

She gave an exaggerated sigh. "Yes. Unfortunately. But I have to say, I'd rather work for her than have her as a member of my family like Anson does. At least I can escape if I need to."

Anson gave a grim smile. "True. I'm stuck with her. Unless she and my brother split, that is. Which won't happen. They're perfect for each other. He lets her lead him around by the nose. They're in it for the long haul."

"Sounds like fun at family gatherings," I said.

He rolled his eyes. "Dude, you don't know the half of it."

Heavy footsteps on the stairs got closer.

Maizy jumped off the sofa. "Hey!" she squealed, running to kiss Cato as he rounded the corner into the room.

I had to say, her unselfconscious affection for all us guys added to the spell she cast over me. She was just so damn guileless.

"Hey, Von," Cato called to me from the doorway after he'd been greeted by Maizy and introduced to Anson. "Looks like we're all here," he said, taking in the scene.

"I guess things get real interesting right about now," I said.

25

MAIZY

THERE I WAS, SURROUNDED BY FOUR GORGEOUS, wonderful, smart men, who for some reason that escaped me, seemed to like me right back.

The chances of my being with one of them by the end of the month, in time for my review and even possibly a promotion, were looking okay.

All complications aside. And there were plenty of complications. Thinking about them broke my heart a little bit.

Like choosing. I shuddered and pushed the thought away.

And here we were at the moment of truth. They were all together at my request, enjoying their cocktails and manly small talk. It was funny, but while I was the hub that pulled all them together, in that moment I also felt like an observer, watching them get to know each other. And they were getting along great, at least on the surface.

Maybe they were being polite for my sake, and they really hated each other?

It would almost be easier if they were rivals. Let a fight break out. Let one of them act like a dickhead. Give me something to dislike. Some animosity would do me a great service.

But there was nothing like that. It was so damn chill.

And I hated myself for wanting anything other than that, just to simplify my life and get my damn promotion. I might have bitched endlessly about my boss Eva, but when it came down to it, was I any better?

But I couldn't dwell on that now. I liked each of these men a lot, and I planned to show them how much.

Classic rock poured out of multiple speakers in the game room. Like the great host that he was, Brade made sure everyone's drink was topped off, and then he plopped onto the sofa beside me, where I draped my legs over his lap. I knew he had household staff, but I'd never seen any of them when I'd been there.

Apparently, money could buy help so good that you never even saw it.

Imagine.

Anson stood. "I'd like to toast Brade, for offering his home for us to gather in."

Brade hung his head in modesty while the room filled with *cheers* and clinking glasses.

He looked up. "My pleasure guys, Maizy. You know, it's actually really nice to hang out with normal people."

"Normal?" I looked around the room, laughing. "We are what you call *normal?*"

Cato furrowed his brow while wearing a huge grin. "I don't know whether to be flattered or insulted."

"Yeah, man. I think the last thing I want is to be normal," Anson added.

"Shit. Okay. What I meant was that it was nice to spend time with people who were not musicians. It's nice to talk about something else for a change," he explained.

I leaned forward on the sofa and cradled Brade's face in my hands. "I'll take normal."

Relieved he'd not insulted anyone, he scraped his messy blond hair back off his face and tucked it behind his ears. His gray eyes said something, but I'd not known him long enough yet to read it with perfect clarity.

I could guess, though.

I looked around the room at my guys, who were all watching me. Von gave me the tiniest nod of his head, and Anson raised his glass to me. That was all I needed. These guys got me hot and bothered and I was going to do something about it. I swung my legs off Brade's lap and slowly stood up, positioning myself right in front of him. I reached back to slowly unzip my pencil skirt, letting it drop to the floor. I moved on to the buttons of my blouse, which quickly joined my skirt in a puddle at my feet. Someone cranked the music a bit louder, and I began to sway. I reached to unhook my bra.

Soon, I was naked save for my nude lace panties and high heels. Brade pulled me close enough to run soft kisses over my tummy, leaving a trail of shivery goose bumps in his wake. I ran my hands through fistfuls of his hair as he reached around to fill his palms with my ass, still pressing his lips to my feverish skin. His hands were those of someone who could play multiple musical instruments—strong, powerful—and were eager to tease something primitive and hungry inside me the way he did to those who listened to his music. He waved behind my back to one of the other guys—which one, I couldn't be sure—and suddenly there were new hands both on me and in my hair, unraveling my braid so waves fell down my back and around my shoulders. Someone inhaled the scent of a handful of it and groaned in appreciation.

I reached for Brade's shirt as another pair of hands moved to my front, pinching my nipples and tugging on my burning tips. I whimpered and tried to wriggle away but was held in place.

By four men.

And I didn't mind. At all.

Good lord. Was this really happening? The last two nights, I'd been with two guys each, and now, I was with *four*? What was I turning into?

Whatever it was, I loved it.

Just like I loved my guys.

Ohmygod. Love?

"Is there such a thing as a *sultan-ess*? Being worshipped by her eager harem?" Anson murmured from somewhere behind me.

It seemed so.

My panties joined the rest of my clothing on the floor, where someone helped me step out of them. I was bent forward until my breasts hung in Brade's face, when behind me, a tongue lapped my slit from one end to the other now that I was folded at a ninety-degree angle.

One finger, and then another, entered my pussy and the sensation nearly drove me over my edge right then and there. I took deep breaths to maintain some modicum of control, digging my fingers in Brade's shoulders to remain upright. He tipped his head back to meet my lips, and I moaned into him as the fingers inside me began pistoning, allowing my juices to run down my inner thighs.

Fuck, these guys were incredible.

Brade pulled back, speaking just loud enough to be heard over the stereo. "Can one of you guys get me a condom from that drawer?" He pointed somewhere in the room, and I whimpered in expectation of what was to come.

I heard someone rustling about. When the condom had been produced, I watched Brade roll it over his brutally hard cock. He pulled me toward him on the sofa, placing one of my knees on either side of his hips. The action spread my legs, leaving me nice and open for him. I reached to run his hard-on through my slick moisture, rubbing him back and forth between my pussy lips, already swollen with anticipation. I could barely breathe, which was fine because all time stopped, anyway. I was completely in the moment, neither thinking back nor ahead. The perfect balance.

And while I was hyperaware that I was about to fuck Brade, it was really as though I were making love to each guy in the room.

Love.

Yup. Love. I loved these guys, each in a different way.

Shit, was I in for a heap of trouble.

Brade's wide crown pushed against me, and I sank onto him, taking the first inch or so he offered.

"Go slow, baby," he said. "I don't want you sore. The other guys might get mad at me for spoiling their night."

Light laughter erupted behind me. It might have been funny, but it was goddamn true. I had to pace myself. We *all* did.

Brade lifted me slightly and lowered me back down, gradually sinking deeply inside me. He stretched his arms along the back of the sofa, gripping cushions until his knuckles were white, his gaze locked on mine. My hands clenched his shoulders for leverage as I began a slow bucking rhythm.

"Hey, baby."

Cato appeared on my left and placed one foot up on the sofa next to me while Brade thrust his hips to meet my bouncing. I reached for Cato's fly, fumbling through his undershorts and trousers until I freed his thick penis. I traced its length with my tongue from the drop of glistening precum on its tip, down to the root where I brushed my fingers around his balls. He sucked in his breath at my contact.

"Taste me," he murmured.

I ground on Brade's cock while I ran my lips over the head of Cato's erection. I glanced up at him, and he looked back at me, I would swear with love in his eyes. I took him deeper in my mouth until I nearly gagged. With two cocks pummeling me, I was a whimpering mess, and with my eyes closed, there was nothing but sensation. Four other hands wandered over my body, one reaching for my clit. As both my mouth and pussy were being fucked with a visceral hunger, my clit was rubbed in hard, quick circles. Like a grand finale, Cato, Brade, and I came within moments of each other, the groans in the room drowning out the music. I rode a beautiful wave of one orgasm after the other, savoring my handsome, sexy guys. With my eyes shut tight, I imagined ways to make them feel just as wonderful. I'd do anything I could for them.

I CAME TO, tucked under a down comforter. For a quick moment, I wasn't sure where I was, but the moonlight coming in the bedroom windows told me I wasn't at home. I looked around, my heart startled into a panicky rush.

Oh. It was Brade's house. Okay.

But where was he? Where were the other guys? *My* guys?

I crawled out of the empty bed to visit the bathroom, and I found the same robe I'd seen the last time I was there. I pulled the plush terry cloth around me and stepped into the hallway, where I could make out soft voices talking about sports, scotch, and a variety of other guy things. I headed for the game room, where I'd last seen everyone.

Standing in the room's doorway, no one noticed me right off. Damn, they were a good-looking lot.

"Hey, guys."

Four heads snapped in my direction. Four very handsome heads, that was.

"Hey, look who it is."

"Sleeping beauty."

"Baby's out of bed."

There were a few other comments, but my head was too fuzzy to track them. I padded over to the sofa, took a seat, and snuggled up to Von. He pulled me to him, planting a kiss on my forehead.

"What's going on? Why was I in bed?" I mumbled, pulling the robe up around my chilly neck.

"I think we wore you out," Anson said with a smile.

"No way." I looked around at each of them.

I was *full* of stamina. What the hell were they talking about?

"He's serious, sweetie," Von said, ruffling my hair. "After our last session, you conked out on the sofa. We put you to bed."

"Huh." I was still out of sorts. "Are you guys doing good here? I feel badly for deserting you."

"We're having a great time," Anson said. "Brade is a killer host, and we're just hanging out."

He made it sound so easy.

But *easy* just wasn't possible. It was supposed to be hard. Shouldn't they hate each other? At least a little? How would I choose?

Could I choose?

26

ANSON

Maizy looked cute as hell when she wandered out of bed and back to the game room where we guys were hanging out. I had to say, we were having a rocking time. They were cool dudes, and it was clear we all cared deeply for Maizy.

I tried not to think about what it might be like when she chose one of us.

But hey, maybe we guys would still be friends?

Actually, probably not. Guys weren't like that.

But perhaps she'd choose more than one of us. Had she even considered that? When I'd shared a woman in the past, it worked out pretty well. That is, until it ended, of course.

Maizy went to get herself a glass of water, and

when she returned, she did not take a seat. Instead, she stood, facing all of us. She looked each of us in the eye for several seconds, saying nothing.

Did she know how much we all cared for her?

"Maiz, are you okay?" Cato finally asked.

She nodded, clearing her throat. "I am. I just have something to say."

"Okay, let us have it," Brade said.

I was glad he pushed her to spill it. I'm not sure I had the balls to.

She took a couple more gulps of water and wiped a drip off her chin with her sleeve. Any other woman, I would have thought was sloppy. But not Maizy. Everything about her captivated me. Smart, beautiful, funny…

"I'm so happy you were all willing to meet. It's been…just wonderful…and I'm thrilled you've hit it off the way you have. Braden, thank you again for hosting."

He raised his glass and nodded. "Happy to."

She turned to Cato, who ran his hand through his hair. "You, Cato, have been such a good friend to me, both at work, and away from work. Thank you." He winked at her and blew a kiss.

"Von. I love your passion for animals. Thank you for helping every creature you get your hands on live a better life." He looked down at his drink for a moment, and then back at her.

And last but not least, she turned to me. "Anson,

thank you for listening to me complain about the trials and tribulations of working for Eva. You've definitely made it more bearable."

What the hell was she getting at?

"Maizy, are you okay?" I asked.

She looked down at her feet, and her face crumbled a bit.

Jesus.

"I...I um...haven't been completely truthful about something." She continued looking down. Whatever was going on, it was tearing her apart. She cleared her throat.

"Well. Here we go," she said. "Cato, you already know a bit about this, but the rest of you do not. My infamous boss, Eva, informed me a couple weeks ago that if I didn't have boyfriend, fiancé, or husband by the time of my review at the end of this month, I would probably be passed over for a promotion."

We all looked around the room at each other.

"They can't do that," Von said. "Can they?"

"Not officially, of course. But she made it clear that when I had a man in my life, the firm would look more favorably on me. As if I'd be more respectable than I am right now, as a single woman."

"You're kidding, right?" Brade asked. "Christ, I thought the entertainment world was fucked."

Maizy nodded. "So I'd hoped to have a guy by the end of the month, in time for my annual review."

I wanted to crawl under a rock, knowing that my sister-in-law was behind this.

Maizy continued. "I just want to say I'm really sorry. I didn't think things would go this far. I never expected to like all four of you the way I do." She sat down and put her head in her hands.

I didn't like seeing her suffer like that. Not at all.

"Maybe I can speak to Eva," I offered. "See if I can talk some sense into her."

Yeah, like she'd listen to me.

Maizy looked at me. "No, no please, Anson. Please don't do that. It would just make things worse."

"It's your call, sweetheart."

"So what are you going to do?" Von asked.

"I have to pick one of you." She gasped as she held back a small sob.

Here we go.

"Of course," she continued, "whoever I pick has to feel the same way about me. And who's to say you will? I could end up alone *and* without my promotion. Actually, that's the most likely scenario."

"What makes you say that?" Cato asked.

She shrugged.

"I don't know. Just my luck, I suppose. Plus, I would think you'd all be disgusted with me at this point, knowing my true intentions."

We looked around at each other. While we might have been caught off guard by Maizy's real plan, I hardly think anyone was disgusted with her.

Although there was a new tension in the air.

Cato crossed the room and took her in his arms, where she stumbled, beginning to sob.

"I'm so sorry," she said, over and over, without moving her face off Cato's shoulder.

So I walked up to them and rubbed her back.

I was furious with my sister-in-law. What the hell did she think she was doing, telling an outstanding woman like Maizy that she was any less than anyone else?

Eva would never be half the person Maizy was. That's all there was to it.

"Maizy, quit that fucking job," I said. Hell, I made enough money for the two of us.

Cato nodded. "Yeah, leave those pricks. *I'm* gonna leave the firm some day, hopefully sooner rather than later."

She shook her head through her tears. "I can't. I need my job. I pay for almost everything for myself and my sister."

I looked around the room. I had the feeling we were each thinking about various scenarios for helping our girl.

I wondered how likely it was we were all thinking of the same one.

"Maiz," I said. "I think I can speak for the group by saying we all care about you. A lot." I looked around to make sure I'd read the other guys as accurately as I'd hoped.

I had.

Cato released her so he could step back and face her. "I think what we're trying to say is that we love you."

27

MAIZY

WHAT THE HELL HAD I DONE?

I'd gotten involved with four guys, knowing I'd have to choose one in the end, and in a short period of time, too.

Now they loved me.

And I loved them right back.

Shit.

I looked around. "You guys are the amazing ones. I...I'm not sure I deserve any of you. I need some time to think. I'm gonna head home for the night."

"You sure, babe?" Brade asked.

I nodded. "I need to clear my head. Thank you for understanding. I...I love you guys, too." There. I'd said it.

I flew to the bedroom where someone had placed

my neatly folded clothes, threw them on, and ran out the door to flag down a cab.

I CRAWLED under the covers as soon as I got home and stripped off my clothes. I even ignored my sister, who was doing naked yoga in the living room.

I felt horrible for bailing on everyone, leaving them there at Brade's house when they barely knew each other, but I'd been suddenly overwhelmed by the knowledge that I held the hearts of four awesome guys in my hands. It was a weighty honor, and one that I in no way deserved. I'd gone through nearly an entire box of tissues when I heard soft knocking at my bedroom door.

"Maizy?" Sparkle asked.

"Come in," I croaked.

She was wearing the robe I'd given her.

She walked over and sat on the edge of my bed. "You gonna tell me what's going on?"

I sniffled hard and nodded.

"I must look like shit," I said, pushing my hair off my face and wiping mascara from under my eyes.

"Yeah. Pretty much."

Why couldn't she scale back on the honesty thing every now and then?

"I can't string these guys along," I moaned. "It's not right."

"Okay. Then which one do you want to be with? Who is your best match?"

That was exactly the problem.

"Anson is funny and snarky, and I love his red hair. Although it is a shame he's related to evil Eva. Brade is sweet as can be and is looking for a life outside touring with his band. Cato has been my savior at work, and I now know he's liked me all along. And you know Von, who saves every animal he can. What's not to love about that?"

"Oooh. You said *love*."

"I did. I do. I love them. I love each of them." The tears welled up again. Shit, I was getting tired of being a crybaby.

"Oh my," Sparkle said.

Oh my was right.

I CALLED in sick to work the next day. I'd never done that before, and I knew Eva would be furious, but for once, I didn't care about pleasing her. I had some serious things to think through, and I needed a damn day off.

I pulled on some yoga pants and sneakers and set out for a long walk.

The city on a weekday was so different from what I was used to. The weekend vibe, when I was usually out and about, had a lot going for it, but I liked the feel of the city with everyone at work or school. I had the place to myself for a change. I liked it. And just as I sat down on a park bench, my cell rang. I jumped to answer it, like the idiot that I was.

"Hi, Cato," I said.

"Hey. You didn't come to work today," he said.

"Yeah. I needed some time. I have a lot on my mind. I'm sure Eva is losing her shit."

"I couldn't tell you. I'm avoiding her like the plague. Look, can you meet me for coffee? Just for a few minutes?"

"Um. Sure."

He gave me the address of a coffee shop several blocks from our office to minimize the risk of running into Eva, and I set off to meet him.

I KNEW WHAT WAS COMING. He was going to tell me to take a hike. That he'd had enough of being jerked around, that I was a horrible friend and a worse co-worker. That I deserved every bit of crap I got from Eva and then some, because I was an awful person, actually even worse than her, truth be told.

Ugh. Why had I agreed to meet him?

But my anxiety slipped out the door the moment I saw him. He entered the coffee shop, a tall drink of water, bespectacled with an expensive, perfectly fitting suit. He turned heads as he moved like a strong, graceful athlete. What a catch. Why had it taken me so long to realize?

"Hey, beautiful," he said, bending to kiss my cheek. "Look at you, all casual in your *sick day* clothes."

I looked down at myself. "Yeah, my sick day clothes."

He sat back in his chair, head tilted, with a small smile, pretty chill for someone who was about to rip me a new asshole.

I stirred a tiny spoon in my cappuccino so he couldn't see how nervous I was and added one more sugar just for something to do.

"How's work for you today?" I asked, not sure what else to say. My head was still reeling from the night before.

"Eh. You know, same as always."

He leaned forward on our small café table, taking hold of my hands.

"So. After you left last night, the guys and I had a talk."

"Uh, okay. A talk about…what?"

"Well, you know, the five of us."

Just what I'd been afraid of. A roiling sensation slammed through my stomach, and I took a deep breath to avoid vomiting all over the arms of his suit.

"Yeah?" I squeaked.

There it was. He'd come on behalf of the group to tell me they were dumping me. I'd end up alone. And of course, with no promotion. I'd still be the firm harlot and Eva's whipping post, no matter how hard I worked, for the rest of my days.

How fucked was *that*? Cato would ignore me at work. Anson would bad mouth me to his evil sister-in-law. Brade would write a song about what a bitch I was that would skyrocket to number one. And Von would send Cher the rat to some other vet to avoid seeing me.

My life would go from being mediocre but generally bearable, to a shitshow of epic proportions.

Even my sister Sparkle would turn on me, furious that I'd let four outstanding men slip through my fingers.

The horror I felt about the life before me must have been written all over my face.

"Maizy, would you relax? You look like someone told you the world was ending in five minutes."

Well, it kind of was.

"We talked for a long time about how we could help you. There's a great opportunity ahead of you at the firm. You could really go far, and we don't want you to let this slip through your fingers."

I shrugged. "It's okay. I'm fine with staying where I am at work. The promotion's not that big of a deal."

Did I really just say that?

"It's not going to happen," I managed to choke out,

"and I've made my peace with that. I was going to try and figure out which of you guys I would be the best match with, but I couldn't do it. I've fallen for all of you. Instead of hurting anyone, I'm not choosing anyone. It's done," I said with authority. "I'm remaining alone, single. On my own."

Did I really believe that?

"Maizy, stop. Just stop," he said, holding up his hand. "You have to choose one of us. We understand, and we want you to be happy. We want you to realize your dreams."

His compassion just about killed me. I jumped from my chair, upending my untouched cappuccino, and made for the door. I didn't need the entire café to witness my explosion of emotion.

Instead, I ran outside so all of Manhattan could see me lose my shit. I was brilliant that way. And Cato was hot on my trail, so when my shoulders began to shake with sobs, he pulled me to him, letting me bury my face in his expensive jacket and cover it with my tears and runny nose.

"Darling. It will all be okay. We're going to make sure it is."

Damn if that didn't make me cry even harder. How in the hell had I earned the respect and affection of four of the most amazing men I'd ever had the pleasure of knowing—and sleeping with?

I pulled a deep breath to get my heaving under control, and as I did, Cato lifted my face to his.

Ugh. I must have looked like shit. But it seemed he didn't care, because his mouth was on me in an instant. The very act of his lips brushing mine had this crazy calming effect I couldn't begin to explain, and my anxiety began to subside. I pulled back to face him, feeling *almost* all right.

Goddamn, he was a magnificent man. I mean, all the guys were, but Cato's quiet, serious way was so powerful. I found him irresistible.

Shit, did he have time to come home with me? Probably not.

His gaze was locked with mine.

"It will be okay. You've got to believe me," he said.

I forced myself to nod. "Yes. Yes, I know. Of course it will be. I just don't want to hurt anyone."

"It is scary. Look, I know I can speak for all the guys when I say this whole thing is goddamn scary. We're feeling it, too. Baby, I've fallen for you. We all have."

Well, there it was. The elephant in the room had just escaped and could never be recaptured.

I was terrified. Could four amazing men really have fallen for me?

But it was no use. I couldn't choose. I wouldn't.

I'd just go back to the grind at the firm. Maybe I'd scale back on how hard I was working, since my efforts seemed to go unnoticed and were certainly not going to be rewarded.

No more twosomes. Or three- or foursomes for that matter.

"I know, it's strange as hell, that four very different guys would all consider you *their type*. But you *are* our type. Honestly," Cato said.

"You're not making this easier, you know."

"It's not easy. That's clear. But we talked about it and are cool with you making a choice. Your happiness is the top priority here, for all of us."

"No. Not choosing. Not gonna do it."

The gravity of releasing them all hurt more than I ever knew it would, but I was determined to do it.

He kissed my temple. "I have to get back to work. Meet us at Brade's tonight. We'll all be there, and we'll figure this thing out together."

I watched him disappear into the throngs of people on the busy Manhattan sidewalk, like a tiny boat getting swallowed by unrelenting waves.

And I stood there, an impediment to the crowds that had just consumed Cato. I didn't care one bit.

28

BRADEN

I'D HAD A BITCH OF A DAY AT THE STUDIO, FIGHTING WITH not only the rest of the band but also our manager and sound engineer.

I had been an insufferable dick, taking my mood out on everyone around me. I owed the guys an apology and made a mental note to take care of that first thing in the morning.

But for now, all I wanted was a cold beer while I waited for Anson, Von, and Cato, and of course, our lovely Maizy.

I'd be lying if I didn't admit I had some trepidation about what might happen when everyone arrived.

Who knew the promise of a little promotion could throw five people into such a state of uncertainty?

The doorbell rang, and I found both Anson and Von had arrived. "Hey, guys. C'mon in."

No sooner had we got to the kitchen when the bell rang again. Von offered to answer the door and returned with Cato.

"Well, here we are," I said, raising my beer bottle.

"Where's our girl?" Anson asked.

"She'd texted me she was on her way." I looked at my wristwatch. "And…she should be here any minute." Just as I said that, the doorbell rang for a final time.

Maizy joined everyone in the kitchen, receiving several sincere compliments.

"Christ, you are gorgeous."

"Yowsa, baby."

"Shit, it's good to see you."

And she *was* freaking beautiful in a short lacy dress and boots that came up over her knees. I was so used to seeing her in work clothes, I couldn't stop staring.

Dude, don't be a dick. Give the girl some air.

But gracious as always, she broke into a giant grin and made her way around the room greeting each one of us. I spotted a hint of sadness in her eyes, but she was working hard to hide it.

She took the champagne I'd poured her. "Okay, guys. Why did you want me to come by tonight so badly? I'm thrilled to see you, but I feel like we all know how this is going to end."

End. That word did not sit well.

"Let's all go up to the game room and get comfortable, okay?" I suggested. In spite of how the evening might have gone, I wanted them all to feel at home in my house.

Once upstairs, Anson stood at the head of the room, having been designated the evening's spokesman.

"Maizy, we have something to talk to you about—"

But she cut him off.

"I've already made my mind up that I'm not choosing. I'll remain single and work will be just fine."

She didn't sound convinced.

"This has been a wonderful, sexy adventure. But I never expected to fall for all of you."

I wasn't an overly sensitive guy, but she was tormented, and that felt like a knife in my heart. I resisted the urge to hold her and tell her everything was going to be okay. Because I didn't know yet if it would.

"And we didn't expect to fall for you, either," Anson said. "But the fact is, we did."

Oh, damn, now tears were slipping down her pretty face. I was a sucker for a crying woman.

Anson continued. "Maizy, we have something to say, and you owe it to us to listen."

Sniffling, she looked around at each of us and nodded, permitting Anson to continue.

"We will always support you, regardless of what happens. We wanted to let you know that, first," he said.

I nodded at Anson for support.

"We want to all stay together. The five of us."

Her brow furrowed in confusion. It was really kind of cute.

"Baby, we want to share you. We could live together or keep our own places. It's up to you."

She looked around at us.

Anson chimed in. "I don't know how that will impact your promotion, or your relationship with my evil sister-in-law, but this is what we want. And we believe it's the best thing for you, too. Think about it for a bit. We believe you'll agree."

The room was silent for what felt like hours. The only thing to be heard was the city traffic in the distance.

"It's okay. I don't have to think about it," she said.

I looked around at the other guys and realized we were all holding our breath to some degree.

The moment of truth.

"I agree with you," she said.

"Agree with what? What do you mean?" I asked.

"I accept your offer." She burst out laughing, and I was across the room like a bolt of lightning, picking her up and laying her back on the thick rug beneath our feet to run kisses up her luscious thighs.

It was time to celebrate, and the other guys were right there with me.

29

MAIZY

HOLY SHIT. I'D EXPECTED TO HEAD HOME THAT NIGHT A single woman. A sad, single woman no doubt, but one with great memories of what it was like to have a man-harem, if only for a very short period of time.

Maybe I'd write a book about it someday.

But instead, they thrust on me the mother of all jackpots.

They *all* wanted me.

They wanted to share me. Who even knew a thing like that existed? I was nervous. I was scared. But I also knew what I wanted, and I was beyond grateful that they felt the same way.

How did I get so damn lucky?

I kissed Braden when he finished tickling my thighs with his lips. He moved aside, and I kissed another guy, and then another. Someone unzipped my boots and threw them aside, and another eased my dress over my head, leaving me in my bra and panties. Those two items didn't last long, either.

I looked up at my men, my beautiful, wonderful men, in various stages of undress gathered around me.

My red-haired Anson was already butt-naked, his cock so heavy that even when erect, it hung down against his thigh.

Cato, my serious boy, was neatly placing his clothes on a chair, and with his back to me, I got to admire his rock-hard ass that quivered just the tiniest amount when he moved.

My animal-lover Von had removed his T-shirt and was sitting on the edge of the sofa stroking the large bulge in his pants.

And last but not least, my rock star Brade, after he'd removed the last of his clothes, stood over me, stroking his hard dick like the man in charge that he was.

And they were all here for me. And of course, I was all in for them.

To hell with the promotion. Fuck Eva and the stupid law firm where I'd sold my soul for too long. Damn those judgmental bores who thought they knew something about me, enough to decide who they thought I was and what they thought I should be.

If only those bitches could see me now. They'd know I was a woman to be reckoned with.

ANSON POSITIONED himself between my legs, putting a pillow under my ass for better access.

"Look at that pretty pussy," he growled. "All nice and smooth for us."

He ran a finger through my slit and brought it back up to his mouth, where he savored my taste.

"Mmmm," he growled, running nibbles up my inner thigh until he reached my swollen lips. His tongue dove between them, dragging along my creamy slit. Someone's mouth had lighted on mine, and I moaned into it, unable to contain the pleasure that was shooting through me.

Anson moved aside with a smile, his shoulder having been tapped by Von, who took his place. Someone else settled on my tits, kissing and sucking them to perfection.

I turned my head to the right and to my delight, there was a hard cock, ready and waiting for me. I opened wide, and Brade buried himself in my mouth nearly to the hilt. My left hand reached out and grabbed another erection, and all my boys were in on the fun.

Four men, whom I loved, were worshipping me in the most intimate way possible, making me moan and scream with a fiery awareness of the love they were offering.

I heard a condom wrapper tear open and a voice ask, "Are you ready for me, baby?" With a mouth full of Brade's cock, Cato on my tits, and Anson in my hand, I moaned for Von to have his way with me. Every inch of my body was being used for pleasure, and it was unlike anything I'd ever dreamt of.

Von drove into me so hard and fast that a burning hot orgasm instantly slashed over and through me. At the same time, Brade pulled out of my mouth and came all over my tits. I arched my back and screamed, pounding my head against the thick rug, my body shaking from head to toe.

"Are you coming, darling?" Anson asked, his lips right next to my ear.

"I…I…want…more," I muttered.

"You heard her, boys," he said, reaching for his own condom.

I managed to open my eyes long enough to see him roll the latex down his thick erection. While he did, Von and Brade each took one of my legs and spread me 'til I was so goddamn open, I thought I might split in half. At the other end up by my head, Cato slapped his cock against my face, alternately letting me have a taste, and then pulling it away.

Before Anson entered me, he bent to tease my hard clit. He flicked my sensitive flesh with his tongue, leaving me writhing in the hands of all the others.

"Please fuck me, Anson. I need it. Please," I begged,

knowing that another release would only whet my appetite for more. I was an insatiable animal.

"Ooohhh," I groaned as he slipped his swollen head just inside me. As he ventured deeper, I moaned for more and opened my mouth so Cato could feed me his hard cock.

Salty precum filled my mouth, and Anson inched deeper inside me. When Von and Brade hoisted my legs higher, my pussy clenched. Waves rolled through me as my guys each marked me in one way or another, and with one last thrust, I tumbled into the most beautiful oblivion a girl had ever seen. The screams I heard must have been my own, even though I wasn't entirely sure, and one after the other, the guys roared with their own orgasms, either coming in or on me. I was covered in hot, sticky cum, weak and mumbling like a fiend.

"I love you," I murmured to the guys, which was met with a return chorus of additional *I love you's* that repeated until it was the last thing I'd heard from the men I gave my heart to. I passed out like I had the night before, thrilled to be in the arms of so much love.

30

MAIZY

HAD YOU TOLD ME HOW DIFFERENT MY LIFE WOULD BE several weeks after that fateful gathering at Brade's, well, I never would have believed you. Life had been a non-stop frenzy of activity, and it seemed like it would never end.

Kind of like my love for the guys. All four of them.

It had all started with Eva. Which was kind of funny, because it all kind of ended with her, too.

And in the end, I didn't mind her that much.

She sauntered by my cube one day the way she did when she was going to ask me nosy, inappropriate questions.

"Say, Maizy. How are things with Anson?"

She asked me this at least once a week.

"Wonderful, Eva. He's a great guy. Why?"

She shifted in her designer pumps, which she didn't even change to commute in, like nearly everyone else in New York did. She actually took the subway in those things.

She looked at the back of her hand and pretended to brush away a speck of lint or dirt.

"Well, it's just that I could have sworn I saw you kissing Cato the other day."

Boom. There it was. She'd finally spit it out. How it must have been eating at her.

And you know what? I could not have cared less. At that point, I wasn't interested in whether she approved of me, liked me, thought I was smart, or the office whore. Nothing. I no longer gave two shits about that sad, narrow-minded woman. And I no longer cared about the law firm or the damn promotion she'd never given me. Fuck her.

"Yes, Eva, I was kissing Cato."

"Um, well, how do you think Anson would feel about that?" she asked.

Clearly, she was ready to take great pleasure in fucking me over by informing him.

"He knows."

She cleared her throat, but it came off as more of a little choking sound.

"What? What do you mean 'he knows'?"

"He knows. The two guys know each other. I'm dating them both." Was it too soon to tell her I was actually dating *four* guys? Or would her head explode?

"Oh."

"Yeah," I said slowly, with my best angelic smile.

"Well, okay. Okay," she said, backing up toward her office like she might catch something from me.

The next day, Cato happened by my desk.

"Guess the cat's out of the bag," he said, smiling.

"What makes you say that?" I asked.

"Looks like it got to the senior partners that you and I are seeing each other. They told me to either end it, or I could leave the firm."

Fuckers.

"So what did you tell them?" I asked.

"That I'd leave the firm, of course," he said.

Good grief, he looked different already. Like he'd hoisted a huge weight from his shoulders. Like he was ten years younger. And like he was a shit-ton happier.

"Um, what? You're leaving the firm?"

"Yes, I am."

TURNED out Cato had been talking to Von about starting a foundation to fund no-kill animal shelters. When they told me about their plan, my heart swelled with pride.

"So, here's the scoop. I'll be the executive director of the organization," Anson said.

"And we'll run it out of my vet office," Von added.

"But we need help," Cato said.

"We need you."

So, I gave my notice at the firm to work with the guys. Anson was quitting his gig to handle the foundation's finances, and Brade was working with his agent to secure a bunch of fundraising concerts that would benefit the organization.

We were just one happy family, thanks in part to Eva.

Who, by the way, had nearly had a heart attack when I told her I was leaving. She really surprised me by taking me to lunch at one of the nicest restaurants in New York City. She'd toasted me with tears in her eyes, leaving me wondering why she'd hidden her nice side with the bitchy façade she was so famous for.

And now I was going to be related to her. Sort of, anyway, through Anson.

CHAPTER 31

MAIZY

"C'mon, guys, we're going to be late."

My jaw just about hit the floor when Cato, Von, and Anson entered our hotel suite's living room, all in elegant black tie.

Holy lord, where did men like this come from?

"Look at *you*," Von growled.

I did a little pirouette for the guys, spinning in my slinky red evening dress that hugged every inch of me to the knees, where it flared out, fishtail-style.

"Daaaamn, baby," Cato said after whistling softly.

Two pair of lips met either side of my neck, but I squirmed away from their temptation just as a hand slithered over my silk-covered ass and pinched me.

"Guys, we gotta get going," I insisted.

"Yo," Anson said, looking at his phone, "the limo's downstairs."

I took a deep breath and looked at the guys. "Let's go. Brade is waiting for us."

The guys helped me climb into the backseat, no easy feat in a long dress and stiletto heels. When we were settled, Anson, who was seated next to me, took my hand as we drove across Los Angeles.

"How'd you get to be so gorgeous, darling?" he asked.

"I might ask the same of you. All three of you," I said, looking from one to the other as we swayed in the rolling limo. Good lord.

Tonight was a big night. Brade was receiving a humanitarian award for his fundraising efforts for the foundation. He insisted that it was really an award for the five of us, but that didn't matter. We would have been there to support him, regardless. There was going to be a celebrity-studded party afterward that promised to carry on 'til the wee hours of the morning. I'd had someone come by the hotel to do my hair and makeup, had bought some crazy-expensive designer dress, and didn't think I'd ever felt so damn good.

We climbed out of the limo into a cacophony of a big, festive party getting underway. Someone with a clipboard waved us toward a red carpet. I was nervous as hell and was petrified of sweating on my dress, but I held my head up like I went to events like it all the time.

Keep smiling, I reminded myself.

The clipboard person pointed to a spot where we were to stop on the red carpet, and Brade appeared out of nowhere to join us. The crowd went wild when they saw him, and he smiled and waved as he took my hand and gave me a kiss on the cheek. He nodded at the rest of the guys, and we all lined up, holding hands like one big happy family. There might have been questions the next day, or even right then, but we didn't care. We were together, and we had nothing to hide.

My four darlings were sharing me.

Cameras flashed in our faces as we smiled, ignoring the questions coming from the press. Well, except for one.

"How'd you get lucky enough to win this award, Braden?" one of the reporters called out.

Brade looked at me, and then the rest of the guys. And I knew just what they were thinking.

It wasn't about luck.

It was about love.

Did you like *The Promotion*?
Check out the next book in the steamy
Contemporary Reverse Harem Collection
THE GALLERY

THE
Gallery
A CONTEMPORARY ROMANCE
Mika Lane

I hope you loved reading this book as much as I loved writing it.
Find all Mika Lane books here:
https://mikalaneshop.com/

Dear Reader:

I'm USA TODAY bestselling romance author Mika Lane, and am OBSESSED with bringing you sassy, steamy stories with imperfect heroines and the bad-a*s dudes they bring to their knees. I'll always bring you my signature humor and heat, topped off with a modern-day happily ever after.

My first book ever was *The Day I Ate the Milkyway*, a true fourth-grade masterpiece illustrated with crayons and bound with construction paper and glue. Nowadays, steamy romance gives purpose to my days and nights as I create worlds and characters that tickle the imagination. I live in magical Northern California with my own handsome alpha dude, sometimes known as Mr. Mika Lane, and two devilish cats named Chuck and Murray.

A dual citizen of the United States and Ireland, I have on more than one occasion spent my last dollar on a plane ticket somewhere, and am always planning my next escape. I often try new recipes on unsuspecting friends, search out hiding places to read undisturbed, and sadly kill every houseplant I bring home.

I LOVE to hear from readers when I'm not dreaming up naughty tales to share. Visit my online shop https://mikalaneshop.com/ and say hello https://mikalaneshop.com/pages/meet-mika.

xoxo, Mika